THE ~~WONDERFUL~~ LIFE OF CONNIE MAGUIRE

DOMHNALL O'DONOGHUE

THE ~~WONDERFUL~~ LIFE OF CONNIE MAGUIRE

MERCIER PRESS

'All characters and events in this book, except for those who are identifiably real and recognisable in the public domain, are entirely fictional. Any resemblance to any person living or dead which may occur inadvertently is completely unintentional'

Mercier Press
www.mercierpress.ie

Published by Mercier Press, 2025
Copyright © Domhnall O'Donoghue, 2025
The moral rights of Domhnall O'Donoghue to be identified as the author of this work have been asserted in accordance with the Copyright and Related Rights Act, 2000.

All rights reserved. This book is copyright material and must not be copied, reproduced, transferred, distributed, leased, licensed or publicly performed or used in any way except as specifically permitted in writing by the publisher, as allowed under the terms and conditions under which it was purchased or as strictly permitted by applicable copyright law. Any unauthorised distribution or use of this text may be a direct infringement of the author's and publisher's rights, and those responsible may be liable in law accordingly.

ISBN: 9781781178713
eISBN: 9781781178720
Audio ISBN: 9781917453448

ABOUT THE AUTHOR

Hailing from Navan, Co. Meath, Domhnall works as a travel journalist, columnist and author. He writes extensively for the Irish and British media, with work regularly appearing in the *Belfast Telegraph, Woman's Way, The Sunday Times* and the *Irish Examiner*. Domhnall has received many prestigious honours for his writing, including the *2025 Travel Extra Travel Journalist of the Year* award.

Mercier Press published his novels *Crazy for You* and *Colin and the Concubine*. His début novel, *Sister Agatha: the World's Oldest Serial Killer*, was published in 2016.

As an actor, Domhnall appeared as Pádraig in TG4's award-winning series *Ros na Rún*.

Dedicated to my parents,
Máire and Seán O'Donoghue

'Surely it is much more generous to forgive and remember than to forgive and forget.'
Maria Edgeworth

PROLOGUE
THEN

'JESUS CHRIST, WHO was driving?'

Jack stared at the woman hidden in the overgrowth and waited for a response. It wasn't forthcoming. When the young Garda began working in the Meath village days earlier, he anticipated rescuing cats from roofs or resolving disputes over unreturned lawnmowers. He never imagined standing in a field at six in the morning where a car had smashed into a tree. The image of the young victim's body, partially shrouded in a yellow raincoat, would stay with him forever. Her arms reached out towards the shattered window as if pleading to live beyond her twenty or twenty-one years. Music blared from a derelict barn, people enjoying themselves, oblivious to the devastation metres away. Jack needed to remove his uniform jacket despite the chilly, autumnal temperatures.

His superior, Sergeant Teddy O'Donnell, knelt beside the middle-aged woman, blood covered her face. Jack couldn't determine what role this mysterious figure had played in the crash: was she an unfortunate witness or the cause of it? He thought about praying, but what use was that now? Pleading with God would hardly bring the girl back to life.

He turned his attention to the road, desperate for the backup to arrive from Navan and Drogheda.

'Where are you, lads?' he whispered. 'Come on, come on.'

Not knowing what else to do, Jack inspected the car again and, thanks to an emerging sunrise, noticed details he'd previously missed. The gleam of the black steel made it seem as if the vehicle had just rolled off the assembly line. The red ribbon sat lopsided on the roof, and the front licence plate read 'MAMMY MAGUIRE'. Was she the woman now desperately pleading with O'Donnell? He marched in their direction but stumbled, not on a branch, as he initially presumed, but on a second lifeless body twisted on the grass.

'Who was driving?' Jack shouted at the woman, the cracks in his voice undermining his authority.

Without saying a word, she removed a necklace and handed it to O'Donnell. The car's headlights caused the blue jewel to sparkle—a glimmer of beauty contrasting the surrounding carnage. He reluctantly accepted it before rising to his feet.

'She was,' O'Donnell mumbled.

'Who's "She"?'

'Concepta. Connie Maguire.'

CHAPTER ONE

NOW

CONNIE MAGUIRE JOLTS awake, gasping for air. She scans the bedroom. Red wallpaper, mould and a list on the door—rules for this guesthouse on Dublin's Gardiner Street, her accommodation since being released from prison.

She remembers a man, drunk and vocal, attempting to enter during the night. There should be a puddle of his urine on the carpet outside. No doubt the proprietor will blame her for his mess.

Twenty-one months after the crash, Connie has yet to shed a single tear. She doesn't deserve that release. But her body has other ways to express her devastation. Pacing the room, she inhales deeply and clicks her fingers to quieten this latest anxiety attack, her lifelong foe.

'Focus on the here and now,' her former counsellor had once advised when discussing these episodes. 'Stop your mind wandering to those dark places. Keep a journal—writing is your friend.'

If she weren't so broken, Connie would laugh, remembering the hours spent filling her notebooks with self-love quotes from inspirational figures like Oprah Winfrey and Dolly Parton.

'If you want the rainbow, you gotta put up with the rain.'

Despite Dolly's claims, rainbows won't change the past, nor will they bring Jess back to life.

One, two, three, four, five.

Connie counts the cigarette burns littering the carpet in another attempt to distract herself, but it's no use. They only remind her of the many stimulants indulged throughout her fortieth birthday party, surrounded by friends and family, as well as influencers and the media.

'The Wonderful Life of Connie Maguire'—the title that foolish journalist planned to call her puff piece on me. If only that were true.

Connie rummages through her scant possessions bunched in a Tesco bag-for-life for something familiar and reassuring but knows she has nothing apart from house keys and clothes that no longer fit her. All her belongings remain in the village. Instead, in her mind's eye, she sees the framed photograph Liam gave her hours before their lives changed forever: mother and son embracing following that early, pivotal rugby match. His face muddied and determined. Her body coursing with pride.

When our lives were full of possibilities.

'It's the photo you've always liked, so I got it framed,' Liam had said on the afternoon of her birthday, handing it to her in the kitchen. 'Those little stones are Swarovski crystals. Is that how you pronounce it? I think that's what Jess said. Anyway, nice, don't you think?'

More than nice, it was perfect.

Connie quickly dresses and grabs her keys and handbag. The paparazzi, determined to document every moment of her post-prison life, have yet to descend. Thanks to 'good behaviour', Connie was released ten months early. She told no one, not even her own son, currently training in the Algarve. Frustratingly, the media somehow knew the exact moment she would pass through the gates of Mountjoy Prison.

'What kind of future can you possibly have?' one reporter provocatively asked. If only she knew the answer. Connie shakes off the memory and flees the guesthouse. All she wants to do is hold that photo again.

She pushes past work-bound pedestrians on her way to the bus depot. Not even a scalding from someone's coffee breaks her focus.

'Look where you're going, you stupid bitch!' the man roars, wiping the Americano from his crisp white shirt.

Connie continues along the street, refusing to give him or anyone else the opportunity to recognise her and mock her wretched state. Once, dark curls cascaded down her back. Now, she sports a tight pixie cut—the premature grey colouring matches her pasty complexion. Her weight has plummeted since that night, and deep dark circles surround her eyes.

Next to the bus depot, she spots a clothing store opening its shutters where she can replace her coffee-stained t-shirt with something bulkier.

Some armour.

CHAPTER TWO
THEN, SATURDAY MORNING

GERRY'S CAFÉ ATTRACTED customers as varied as the dishes on the menu, thanks to the many festivals and events in the region. The eponymous owner capitalised on the increased footfall in the village by inviting artists, farmers and producers to sell their wares. They filled the adjacent courtyard, which previously had no purpose other than growing moss or playing host to rats, growing fat from the contents of rubbish bins.

Connie, dressed in combat trousers, toyed with her ponytail and waited for Gerry to return with her cake. Today, she ushered in a new decade and would soon throw a garden party to mark this milestone and celebrate the news making headlines nationwide. After shining on the provincial rugby team, her only child, Liam, had made Ireland's national squad. Years of attending punishing training academies had finally paid off. Only a select few could handle the ups and downs of competitive sports, and her son was one of them. Connie would constantly credit Liam's grandfather for his drive and steely focus.

'Those traits must have skipped a generation because he certainly didn't inherit them from me!' she would joke, much to Liam's annoyance.

What was to be an intimate birthday celebration was turning into a major event, with the number of guests mushrooming by the minute, and Connie needed help in the form of a large cake. Her father, recently bedbound following a nasty infection, would be there, accompanied by his new carer. Less positively, Connie had just received a text from Breege, the mother of Liam's girlfriend, Jess.

'We'll bring a few friends and a beer keg and make it a night to remember!'

Connie adored thoughtful and quick-witted Jess, and it brought her constant delight and comfort that she was in her son's life. The young woman wasn't cut from the same cloth as her mother, who caused destruction everywhere she went. A night out with Breege invariably turned sour, and she regularly frequented the Garda station, her knuckles bandaged after punching somebody in The Steeples pub.

'Happy birthday, Ms Maguire!'

Connie spun around. Eli Wall, a child from the school where she worked as a special needs assistant, stood at the door, holding a bouquet.

'They aren't for me, I hope.'

'Yes! They're from our class. Everyone gave a euro.'

'A euro? Now, why would you do something like that? I suppose I'll have to bring in some cake on Monday, won't I?'

Delighted, he hugged her tightly and whispered, 'We love you, Ms Maguire, but I love you the most!'

'By the way, Eli!' Connie called out as he returned to his parents waiting outside, 'I heard you fell last night.'

He looked at her, confused. 'What? I did not.'

'Fell asleep!' Connie could never resist a corny joke.

The sweet gesture of flowers reminded her to get Liam something to mark his success. She spotted a stand in the courtyard with wooden champagne boxes alongside chopping boards and wind chimes. She approached the carpenter, fielding birthday greetings and 'you must be a proud mammy' comments from well-wishers, and requested the inscription: 'Congratulations, Liam—have a *ball*'. She may have been a decade older, but her humour remained as childish as ever.

'Hey, birthday girl!'

It was Mary Elizabeth. Connie always claimed you'd hear her best friend before seeing her, which was saying something considering her peroxide-blonde hair and elaborate outfits. On stage, being watched, was where this amateur actor felt most comfortable, which explained why she and Connie were so close: opposites attract.

'Time for a quick coffee inside, sweetie?' Mary Elizabeth asked. 'There's something you should know.'

Connie rarely took her friend too seriously, but now she was concerned. 'Okay, I need to collect Liam's present first. I'll follow you in.'

'A cappuccino?'

'Skimmed milk. I can't abandon my diet, not even today.'

'Sweetie, you'll need full-fat when you hear the news. I'll get you a pastry as well. Lots of cream.'

* * *

'I see.' Connie sipped her cappuccino, allowing her best friend's revelations to settle. 'Well, I suppose he's every right to be there.'

'Stop!' Mary Elizabeth shot back. 'Don't dare defend him after everything he's done. Or not done. You don't always have to whip out the guitar and sing "Kumbaya" around the campfire, you know, Connie. It's okay to be angry. That bastard has *no* right to be there, swanning in when it suits, cock-of-the-hoop. And having the gall to bring some trollop with him!'

Connie scanned the café; the many animated conversations meant her best friend's fury went unnoticed.

'How many training sessions did he take Liam to?' Mary Elizabeth continued, the coffee rousing her spirits further. 'How many sweaty, muddy jerseys did he wash? How many matches did he attend, and how many words of encouragement did he shout from the stand? Exactly.

And now, the very week Liam makes the national team, he thinks he can just swoop in.'

'Seriously, it's okay that Nick's coming,' Connie lied. 'It's important that Liam has a relationship with his father. It might help centre him now that he'll be in the spotlight more than ever.'

'Do you honestly think Nick has returned because he wants Liam to remain grounded? He wants his share of the spoils, to be part of the glory.'

'That's enough now. You've made your point.'

But Mary Elizabeth had barely begun making her point. 'I wouldn't be surprised if he started tapping him for money or tickets to the Six Nations or World Cup. Or, more likely, VIP passes into nightclubs where he can take advantage of young, impressionable women like—'

'Like me?'

Mary Elizabeth shrugged.

'So, when is he arriving?' Connie asked after a moment, toying with the chocolate sprinkles on the rim of the cup.

'He's already here,' Mary Elizabeth whispered, having spotted some busybody eyeing them from behind his menu. 'That's what Jess told me in the pharmacy just now. Oh, by the way, I've told her to do your nails later. We need you looking red-carpet fabulous.'

'No matter what you throw on me, I'll look like the Wreck of the Hesperus.'

'Stop!' Mary Elizabeth cut in. 'None of that talk. You're absolutely beautiful.'

'If you say so. Has Nick—'

'Been over to your house? About half an hour ago, although he refused to go in. Liam had to come out into the garden. Imagine. Jess mentioned he had a present to say congratulations. Probably something he bought in a euro store. Or stole somewhere.'

'Is he staying with his brother?'

'Yeah. I wonder who she is, this girlfriend. She'll soon learn his ways.'

Connie's insistence that she was comfortable with Nick's sudden return starkly contrasted with what she truly felt. Before becoming pregnant with Liam, she'd spent most of her teenage years willing Nick to pay her attention, but he was too cool to even look at her. Then chance threw them together. The sixteen-year-old found him suffering a seizure on the village square, and stayed with him until his convulsions stopped.

Nick was a year older than Connie, and her crush blinded her to rumours that he had one thing on his mind. When they later bumped into each other at a funfair, Connie couldn't believe her luck when he bought her candy floss before asking her to join him on the Ferris wheel. Later, they had consensual but rough sex behind the rugby pitch's dressing rooms. Not that Nick was interested in Connie, and he relished telling her as much after the announcement of her pregnancy.

'Listen, "Connie with the Ronnie",' as he'd suddenly nicknamed her. 'I was only interested because that uptight prick Teddy O'Donnell fancied you, and I thought it'd be a laugh. Do you think I want to have a baby and settle down? With you, of all people? Jesus, Con!'

Nick had no desire to get trapped in 'this dull dump', so following the news of imminent parenthood, he disappeared to New York before eventually returning to Dublin. Every four or five years, there were sightings at Christmas, but ultimately, he'd been a stranger to the village and his son.

Connie's next battle was with Helga, her German mother, who immediately raised the subject of midnight ferry crossings to England.

'I thought the church said abortion was a sin, *Mutter*. But now you want me to head over to Liverpool and get one? How does that work? Tell me!'

'You will be shunned—*I* will be shunned!' her mother fired back in the Bavarian accent she never lost despite living in Ireland since the seventies when she arrived as an au pair. 'How could you do this to me? You dirty, dirty *schlampe*!'

Connie refused to follow the priest's insistence to heed her mother's 'tough but well-meaning' advice. Much to Frau Maguire and Father Ryan's dismay, the teenager harboured a profound contempt for Catholicism and its embarrassment of hypocrisies. She could never reconcile Jesus' encouragement to 'love thy neighbour' with the church's less gracious reinterpretation to instead 'judge and shame and humiliate and marginalise and control thy neighbour'. Notably single mothers. No, full of determination, Connie insisted she would keep her baby regardless of her 'fall' in status, a decision that brought her untold joy after giving birth months later.

Things became complicated when Liam entered double digits and demanded a father-son reunion. Initially, Connie was lukewarm about a meetup, but when a teacher linked Liam's outbursts in the classroom to Nick's absence, she reluctantly gave her blessing. However, after a night bowling in Dublin, followed by burgers in a greasy takeaway, Nick decided against forging a long-lasting relationship with his son. After this first get-together, Liam's messages and phone calls went unanswered, breaking Connie's heart all over again. According to Mary Elizabeth, Nick was finally organising a follow-up date thirteen years later.

He was never a man to be rushed, Connie thought as Gerry placed her cake and a plate of cream pastries on their table.

'Actually, Gerry, you can take those pastries back,' Mary Elizabeth instructed her older brother, 'Connie needs to look even more gorgeous than usual and show that bollocks what he's been missing out on.'

'You're talking about Nick?' Gerry asked, removing the plate from the table. 'I saw him passing the square earlier, talking to anyone who'd listen. He, eh …'

'He what, Gerry?' Mary Elizabeth had no interest in formalities.

'He'd a woman with him.'

'We heard.' Mary Elizabeth spat out the words. 'She's hideous looking, I bet.'

'I have to say she was—'

'Hideous.'

'Yes, Mary Elizabeth—hideous. Revolting. Like something from a horror film.'

'Do you know what's not hideous and revolting and like something from a horror film? These,' Connie interrupted, swiping a puff pastry from the plate. 'Besides, I think this is exactly how it should be. It's Liam's day.'

'And your big birthday.'

'And his father should be here to cheer him on.'

'You deserve to be sainted, Connie Maguire!' Mary Elizabeth teased. 'I'll even send the paperwork to the pope myself!'

Connie laughed, swallowing the pastry past a lump in her throat.

CHAPTER THREE

NOW

CONNIE SITS AT the front of a bus, gripping her handbag. Her newly purchased scarf, cap and coat are ill-suited for the summer heat. It has been twenty-one months, one week and two days since she was last in the village. Now that her earlier anxiety attack is giving way to a modicum of clarity, Connie recognises the many flaws in her plan to return. If spotted, which is all but guaranteed in a small community, she can no longer call upon the two men in her life for support. With the World Cup on the horizon, Liam is at a training camp with the Irish rugby team in the Algarve while her father died soon after her sentencing. The trial was over quickly—Connie pleaded guilty—but she remains convinced that the events of that night caused her father's rapid decline into dementia.

Though granted compassionate leave to attend the funeral, Connie feared that her presence, handcuffed and surrounded by police officers, would become the focus. Her kind father didn't deserve that. He was the one who had defended her, his only child, when she revealed her shock teenage pregnancy. He was the one who had challenged Connie's late mother when she demanded that the 'dirty *schlampe*' be kicked out of the house.

The bus abruptly stops outside the village after a truck bullies its way from a side lane onto the main road. Through her sunglasses, Connie glimpses the rusty roof of Kavanagh's barn, taunting her through the trees. The scene of the crash.

When he last visited her in prison, Liam had made her vow not to fall back on old habits upon release. She didn't need persuasion. Connie could have easily convinced a doctor to write her a prescription, just as she had done so often in the past. But this convicted killer no longer deserves the calming benefits of Xanax or Valium or any mood-enhancing medication.

Connie kicks an empty can along the floor, hitting a passenger walking to the front. The man, dressed in paint-splattered overalls, glances at her—twice.

I recognise him.

Instead of attacking her, he smiles before crossing the road towards a construction site beside the wood.

'Buses can't drive into the square this month because of roadworks,' the driver roars as if to a stadium instead of a handful of scattered passengers. 'Anyone else for the village should get out at the petrol station up ahead. And if you're heading back to Dublin, pickups are now across the road.'

Connie surveys the traffic through the window, with cars driven by former neighbours, friends and colleagues. 'Enemies' would now be a more suitable description. The driver eventually pulls into the petrol station in front of its unmistakable mascot: the brave inflatable lion that has been exciting children for almost two decades, including a younger Liam. Connie adjusts her scarf and fixes her sunglasses. Her return to the village this morning isn't courageous. It's idiotic and dangerous.

I need to get my photograph.

CHAPTER FOUR
THEN, SATURDAY MORNING

DETERMINED THAT THE party wouldn't descend into an episode of a trashy soap, Connie channelled her energies into something productive: cleaning her already spotless house.

Nick has every right to be here.

There weren't many silver linings about her father's dementia, but at least he wouldn't be aware of Nick's presence here today. Otherwise, to quote the Sophie Ellis-Bextor song blaring from the radio, there'd be murder on the dancefloor. Even though she had begged him not to, her father visited Nick's family several times in those early months. Not hoping to achieve some shotgun wedding—he knew that Nick was a bad egg and had little interest in having him as a son-in-law—but to demand that the family paid its fair share.

'I want to do this on my own, Dad!'

'Fine words butter no parsnips,' he had replied—it was one of his favourite expressions. 'Besides, they've enough money with that big house of theirs. And all those cars.'

Nick's parents, disgusted by Connie's 'condition' and used to getting everything their way, reluctantly contributed financially, but when Liam was born and didn't receive their surname, relations between the families soured. As the years progressed, there had been a truce, and Liam spent time in his grandparents' house, learning the ropes of their profitable family business, school uniform manufacturing. Then, the seven-year-old returned distressed one evening after overhearing Nick's parents discuss Connie in a less-than-flattering light, and the afternoons spent in their clothing factory petered out. The many scholarships Liam subsequently received allowed him to pursue his passion for rugby without their financial support. Since then, the two families had remained cordial, but Connie always bristled when they bumped into each other in the village.

Yes, her father's illness was devastating, cruel and unfair, but at least it would allow Nick to remain injury-free. She spritzed cleaner across the window. After wiping the glass, she jumped, startled by a figure in the garden.

'Teddy! You frightened me!'

'I'm sorry, Concepta, that wasn't my intention. I should have called ahead.'

'Don't mind me. I'm a little on edge today. You know what it's like ahead of a party.'

'As it happens, I've never thrown one, but I can imagine.'

With a dull complexion and personality to match, Teddy was one of the area's four gardaí, a position that perfectly suited his earnest, forthright nature. He was so ordinary, it almost made him extraordinary. There were three loves in his life: rules, rugby and, since primary school, Concepta, as he continued to call her. Despite repeated efforts at igniting a romance, the police sergeant had reluctantly settled for friendship with his former classmate. First dibs on tickets to Liam's rugby matches helped ease the heartache.

'I'm on duty all day and night,' Teddy reported, his melancholic voice matching his dejected expression, explaining that Jack, a recent addition to the team, was still learning the ropes. 'So, regrettably, I won't be able to make your party.'

'Ah, I'm sorry to hear that—you'll be missed.'

'Looks like I'm pretty popular at the moment,' Teddy proudly announced, running his hand through the few remaining hairs on his round, weathered head. 'Simon Wall, the construction manager of the building site, has just invited me to a party out west.'

'What a coincidence, his gorgeous son gave me a bunch of flowers over in the café,' she replied, pointing to the vase on the coffee table bursting with marsh orchids, bluebells and rhododendrons.

'They're certainly making their mark around the village. Well, I suppose they can afford to be generous—Simon owns a few properties in Navan and Trim.'

'And where's their party, Teddy? If I'd known, we could have joined forces, and my hands wouldn't be red-raw from scrubbing the house.'

'In a caravan park, if you don't mind! That probably doesn't sound glamorous to a lady like you, Concepta, especially as the park seems to have passed its glory days. No hot water in the showers or taps, for instance, broken windows, you know what I mean. But, according to Simon, it has some of the best views in the country.'

'I'm not sure if I could live without hot water, Teddy, but I bet it's very peaceful out there, being so close to the Atlantic.'

'Not with twenty-odd drunken builders, I wouldn't imagine. Besides, as nice as it was to be included, especially considering I'm no more than a stranger to him, I wondered whether the fellow was trying to sweeten me up in case he needed a favour down the line. Maybe I'm doing him an injustice, but to quote my late grandmother, it's better to err on the side of caution. Accepting gifts or invitations isn't my style, as I hope everyone knows. You'll be pleased to learn I turned him down without hesitation.'

'Good for you. But all's not lost—I'll save you a slice of birthday cake. Don't interpret that as a bribe, do you hear? I won't be asking you for any favours! So, call around when you're free, and I'll fill you in on all the sordid details from today's party!'

'I'd like that very much, Concepta—I really would!' He made no efforts to hide his enthusiasm. 'Not the sordid details, though—I'm not a gossip—but having cake with you. That would be nice.'

'That's settled, then. Instead of a slice, I'll upgrade it to a slab. How's that? And we can talk about non-gossipy things.'

'Something to look forward to. I'm sure I'll see Liam soon to congratulate him on his success.' His voice cracked with emotion. 'I never doubted him.'

'You never did.'

'As you probably know, it's been the lead story on LMFM all morning. The Meath County Council will soon be commissioning statues of him for the village square. Maybe they'll put it in the middle of the fountain. Wouldn't that be something?'

'Without sounding like one of those pushy mammies, I never doubted that he'd make it, either. It shows that you reap the rewards when you put in the effort. Sure, look at you!'

'Only you can make everyone feel like an international sports star, Concepta! There's a lot to celebrate in this house today, that's for sure.' Teddy suddenly shifted uncomfortably. 'God help me if Nick does anything to ruin it. I assume you heard he returned. Convenient timing, if you ask me.'

'That's what Mary Elizabeth said.'

'I hope he doesn't cause a scene.'

Connie smiled, grateful for his concern. 'We're all going to have a lovely day. I know it.'

Teddy nodded, not entirely convinced. 'Anyway, I'd best be making tracks. I have to call into the Waldrons' house in the wood and plead with Mandy to stop hoarding so much junk in the garden.'

'One man's treasure, as they say.'

'I suppose, but how the surrounding trees haven't caught fire is beyond me. It's a deathtrap. Making matters worse, I believe Mandy adopted a new dog, and her sister isn't pleased. The barking is non-stop.'

'And I'm sure the dog is being vocal as well,' Connie teased. It took Teddy a moment to understand the joke.

'Barking, the sister. Very good. Oh, I almost forgot,' he said, handing her a box. 'For your birthday. It belonged to my late grandmother—the one who said it's better to—'

'Err on the side of caution.'

'That's the one. You deserve everything and more.'

And with that, he hurried down the driveway. After watching his car speed out of view, Connie opened the box to find a silver necklace with a brilliant blue sapphire, her birthstone.

'Oh, my word.'

While she had never been in love with him, Connie certainly loved Teddy like a brother. He had showered her with a profusion of treats over the years, but this gift was different. She placed it around her neck and allowed her curls to fall onto her shoulders.

'Princess Connie,' she whispered, adopting a clipped regal accent. 'I could get used to this!'

'Where's the birthday girl?'

Liam emerged from his bedroom, dressed smartly in a navy blazer, chinos and an open-collared shirt. His sartorial choices were almost unseen behind a mound of red roses.

'I hope they're not for me,' she said. 'You know you shouldn't be wasting your money like that.'

'You think a lot of yourself, don't you? They're for my personal chef, my personal cleaner, my personal shopper! The president of my one-person fan club! My biggest supporter! They're for the most beautiful woman in all of Leinster!'

'No wonder Jess can't resist your charms!'

He handed her the roses. 'If I had my way, Mother dearest, you'd receive flowers every day, which will be the case when those big pay cheques start rolling in!'

'You and your silver tongue—you didn't get that from me, that's for sure!'

Liam shifted awkwardly. 'Sure you're okay with Dad coming later?'

'He's your father, and he'll always be welcome in this house.'

'When he called in earlier, I could tell he was proud of me.'

'He is proud of you. We all are. Now, before your success goes to your head,' she added, handing him a brush, 'can you give the kitchen floor a little sweep? I better get ready. Oh, I almost forgot—look at this stunning necklace Teddy just gave me. Isn't he so thoughtful? It belonged to his late grandmother.'

'It's beautiful. As we're on the subject of gifts, I've something else for you.'

He removed a photo frame from his blazer pocket. The photograph revealed a younger Liam wrapping one arm around a trophy and another around his proud mother. 'It's the photo you've always liked, so I got it framed. It mightn't be as glamorous as Teddy's necklace, but those little stones are Swarovski crystals. Is that how you pronounce it? I think that's what Jess said. Anyway, it's nice, don't you think?'

She examined the photograph. That match seemed like it took place yesterday and also a hundred years ago. His performance on the pitch that day had wowed the crowd. Even though the dream of being a professional rugby player had already calcified in his bones, that was the match when everyone, including the three scouts in attendance, realised that he possessed the talent needed to reach the top of the game. That afternoon, several training academies and private schools offered him scholarships, marking the start of a new trajectory in his career. It was why the photograph had always meant so much to Connie, and it leaned against the dressing-table mirror in her bedroom. Now, with a gorgeous new frame, her son had given the memento the festooning it richly deserved.

'I'll cherish it. I love it. And I love you.'

'Nowhere near as much as I love you.'

Connie needed a moment to compose herself. 'Remind me to give you something I picked up in the market, something small. Right, I must get ready. I better fit into my new dress. I didn't get down—'

'"The weight like I hoped I would." Mam, if only you realised your weight has always been the least interesting part of you. If you were the size of this cottage, which you aren't, by the way, before you start thinking you are, but if you were, you'd—'

'Still be the most beautiful gal in the village.'

'The most beautiful gal in the village.' Liam gently took her by the hands. 'I know I've said this to you before, but if only you loved yourself half as much as we all do.'

'That will be my resolution for the decade ahead. "New beginnings," as they say.' She looked at the clock again. 'Right, that shower won't take itself.'

'Why don't you have a soak in the bath instead? It'll relax you.'

'I don't have the time. I've cream to whip, and I've to give the tiles a quick wipe. And I've cream to whip.'

'You already said that. I'll do those things. Make the most of me while I'm still here.'

'If you're sure. When you finish the floor, would you be an angel and put your roses in a vase? There's a second one under the sink.'

'Aye, aye, Captain! Now, run your bath!'

'And the rubbish! Will you bring the bin out? But don't dirty your clothes either. And don't whip the cream too long or it'll curdle.'

'Consider it all done. Now, off you go!'

Connie smiled as she watched her son work, remembering when teenage Liam hated being asked to help with the domestic chores.

If only his younger self could see him now.

CHAPTER FIVE
NOW

CONNIE FAILS, FOR the third time, to unlock the front door. She peers into the front window of her thatched cottage, hidden at the end of a lane. The net curtains make it impossible to see anything within, but as Liam has previously paid two years' rent in advance, there's no reason to suspect everything isn't the same. Well, not exactly the same, she thinks, recalling the graffiti emblazoned across the walls or the many rocks fired through the windows in the immediate aftermath of that night. Fleeing to Liam's new apartment in Dublin until her sentencing had probably saved her life.

After creeping around to the back garden, Connie's hands and legs shake, recalling where every one of the hundred invited and uninvited guests sat, danced or took photographs during her birthday. At least until she locked herself in the bathroom and passed out.

The pills.

The alcohol.

The barbecue.
The argument.
The interview.
The blind date.
The phone call.
The vixen.
The crash.

Connie holds onto a chair, allowing the memories to wash over her. It takes her a moment to realise the garden furniture is new. So, too, are the toys scattered across the patio. Through the back window, she sees that someone has transformed the kitchen. Bright blue paint has replaced her vibrant Moroccan tiles, while the pine presses have made way for flashy glass cabinets.

'Who the hell are you?' a bearded man shouts, appearing inside the kitchen, a pregnant woman standing behind him. Before Connie can say a word, a look of recognition crosses their faces.

'Don't mind my husband, Connie,' the woman says, emerging into the garden. 'It is Connie, isn't it? You become overprotective when you've children, don't you? God, sorry, that came out wrong. I didn't mean to offend you.'

'I heard on the radio that they released you early,' the man interrupts, joining them. 'It must feel good to be free.'

The woman nudges him.

'What? I've never met anyone who's been to prison before. Especially for something as horr—'

'I'll go,' Connie cuts in. 'I didn't know my son had given away my house.'

'Didn't the landlord tell you?' the woman asks. 'Do you know where your belongings are?'

'It's fine. There's nothing I want apart from something sentimental.'

'I can't believe he didn't tell you. Let me call him.'

'Don't worry about it. I'm sure someone told me. I must have forgotten.'

'Do you need clothes or toiletries? Why don't you come in?'

'No, I'm fine, thank you. There was only one thing I needed, but I'll have to do without it.'

The woman places a hand on Connie's arm. 'It was a horrible thing that happened that night, but it was complicated. Jesus, I've had my own difficulties with, you know, mental health.'

'Have you?'

'After my first arrived, I could barely leave the house. I cried more than he did. The crash on the night of your birthday wasn't as the papers made out. Bastards. It's because you and your son are famous, I'd say, and they wanted the headlines. Anyway, I hope you can start somewhere else. Although probably not here. That's why I'd say we got your house. I suppose everyone assumed that you'd stay in Dublin. Not that you can't come back, of course.'

The man mumbles something under his breath. Connie imagines he disagrees with his wife's sentiments. She looks at the garden one last time. Flashbacks from her birthday. The same flashbacks that have burned through her mind during the past twenty-one months. Without saying another word, an empty-handed Connie turns and leaves along the side of her home. Her former home.

CHAPTER SIX

THEN, SATURDAY AFTERNOON

WITH THE WATER losing its heat and knowing her guests would soon arrive, Connie got out of the bath. Anxious nerves had been replaced with the giddy variety. The canary-yellow maxi dress and white cardigan she'd recently purchased with Mary Elizabeth hung on the bedroom door. They'd made a day out of it, driving together to Dublin for the end-of-summer sales. Without her best friend's encouragement—'it makes you look like an influencer, sexy and chic!'—she probably would never have bought the dress. It was the most appealing option from Mary Elizabeth's many suggestions that day, which included a tiger-print miniskirt and leather pants.

She dressed, adding a belt and spritz of Italian perfume onto her neck. Examining herself in the mirror, she didn't hate what stared back at her.

This feels like a new beginning, she thought, looking at the framed photograph of herself and her son on the dressing table. *Yes, a new beginning.*

'Mam!' Liam called from the kitchen, 'Jess is here to do your nails!'

'I'm coming out now!'

As the words escaped her mouth, Connie felt her voice go. She held onto the doorknob as a heaviness pressed down on her. She turned and stared at herself in the mirror again, trying to determine what was happening. Just a moment before, she'd been genuinely pleased with her reflection. Why did she now feel uncomfortable in her skin? Why did she want to cry? And vomit? Her palms felt sticky. Her face blanched, and her breath verged on a wheeze.

Connie couldn't bring herself to open the door and join her son. Her clouded mind attempted to make sense of this ugly situation. She had already accepted Nick's return. Or maybe it was thoughts of being the centre of attention. She had always spurned the spotlight, preferring to play a supporting role instead. A supporting role to Liam, to Mary Elizabeth, to her father.

It's really Liam's day, she reasoned, failing to steady her hands. *The focus will be on him.*

Was that it? She hadn't properly processed the less positive outcome of his success. Was she frightened about being alone for the first time in her life? Liam had insisted on attending a prestigious grammar school in Drogheda as a day student, even though his scholarship entitled him to be a boarder. Later, despite several teammates offering him a spare room in Dublin, he commuted to Donnybrook while training with the Leinster squad. Now, at twenty-three years of age and a member of the national team, he was finally moving out for good. It was inevitable, she knew, but that didn't make the realisation any easier to accept. Mary Elizabeth had often warned that 'mothers, whose children are their entire world, will be in for a shock when they suddenly find themselves alone'. She started sweating. A telltale rash snaked across her décolletage. All the benefits of her relaxing bath had disappeared. She was back in familiar territory.

New beginnings, remember? New beginnings.

No matter how difficult today would prove for her, Connie was determined not to return to those years of lying, stealing, forging and concealing. She had come too far. The medication hidden inside a slit in her mattress was only there to reassure her. She never intended to take those tablets again, not after all the promises she had made to her son. In the past three years, she hadn't even been tempted once.

Until now.

She grabbed her yoga mat and lay down on it. As she'd done many times in the local fitness studio, she repeated a mantra and attempted to ignore the wicked voice inside her head.

Return to the breath.

She placed her hands on her stomach, filling it with air like a balloon. On an exhale, she released a long sigh, and between exhalations, vocalised all the phrases so often used in class.

'Open your heart.'

'Express gratitude.'

'Invite love to flood in.'

'Everything all right in there?' Liam called from the hall.

'Fine, give me a minute!'

The wave of heaviness and sadness worsened as if she were being dragged to the ground.

Don't, she pleaded with herself, desperately trying to avoid the lure of her mattress. *Don't. Not after coming so far.*

But she couldn't do it alone today. No matter how many deep breaths she took or mantras she repeated, Connie couldn't face her guests unaided. Slowly, she reached her arm under her mattress.

CHAPTER SEVEN
NOW

CONNIE KNOWS SHE should never have returned to the village, but her decisions weren't her own this morning. Waiting for the bus to arrive, she shelters in the old telephone box on the square, where she regularly called Mary Elizabeth as a teenager to discuss the day's events, even though they had spent the entire day together at school. Using the home phone was one of many privileges her parents didn't extend to her. The cramped space is now lined with second-hand books, which affords her additional coverage from prying eyes. She looks at her watch for the umpteenth time.

Where is this bus?

Through a gap between novels by Claire Keegan and Emily Hourican, she stares at the church of St Gerard Majella, her mother's home from home. Another favoured pastime of Connie and Mary Elizabeth was to ignite every candle on the wrought-iron stand, ignoring the sign that demanded ten-pence donations. In recent years, they introduced battery-operated alternatives, and the recommended donation soared to a euro. Even so, devout parishioners continued to use them, foolishly hoping their prayers would be answered by twisting a cheap device.

In prison, Connie's parole officer encouraged her to visit the chaplain.

'It would look favourably on you.'

After years of hating the church, she agreed, albeit reluctantly. The man's accented voice was fragile, his manner uncertain, and his slight frame struggled to fill the black robe.

'Would you like me to hear confession?'

Connie instinctively shook her head; after all, she had already confessed to the worst crime imaginable, and the facts would remain unchanged no matter how many times she revealed what happened that night, whether in a public courthouse or a private confessional.

'When you die, is it the end?' she probed after a moment, a question that had been whirling in her mind every moment since the crash.

'It's only the beginning for them,' he assured her. 'The church teaches us about individual judgement, which happens at death. God will judge us on how we've lived our lives.'

'Jess barely had a life!' Connie snapped. 'She was kind and caring to everyone she met. She loved and was loved in return, especially by my son. Why does anyone have to judge her?'

'Then, from what you say, she lived her brief life following God's teachings. Her soul will certainly go to heaven.' After a moment, he added: 'And rest assured, life will eventually get easier for you and your son without Jess. God never gives us more than we can handle.'

'Then how cruel your God is.'

Not for the first time, Connie now turns her back on the church. Directly in front of her is the café. According to Liam, Gerry made good on his promise to sell the business and move to Marbella with his Spanish husband and their two children. Heartbroken by that night, Mary Elizabeth joined them but vowed to return to Ireland the minute Connie was released. Before uprooting to Andalusia, the siblings had attempted to visit her in prison. Not that Connie ever agreed to meet with them. She didn't want anyone to see her there, dressed in uniforms that had to be repeatedly changed, given the shocking speed at which her weight plummeted. Since childhood, Connie had struggled to lose those 'pesky few pounds', as she had referred to them, but never imagined achieving her lifelong goal following an eighteen-month incarceration.

Apart from an unfamiliar server mopping the floor, only one person is visible in the café, devouring an Irish breakfast. Like the telephone box and cottage, the space has undergone a dramatic reimagining. The tables are glass rather than wooden, and the previous mocha paint has made way for a less welcoming shade of silver. Instead of eclectic work by local artists, the main wall now showcases just a single painting, a lighthouse. Connie studies it, admiring the white structure's fortitude against the belligerent waves.

Despite these aesthetic changes, Connie vividly recalls where she sat, chatting to Mary Elizabeth, sipping cappuccinos and devouring pastries. How differently her birthday would have played out if her best friend had not shared the news about Nick. What if Liam's father hadn't returned to the village? Suppose he hadn't wanted his 'share of the spoils', as Mary Elizabeth had described it.

Jess would still be alive.

Indulging in these hypothetical scenarios had tormented Connie since the crash. She constantly visualised situations that would have resulted in a different outcome—one where that chilling phone call never came, forcing her to leave the cottage and storm the roads to the barn. But nothing, especially these exhausting fantasies in her head, can change the past.

'Returning here wasn't your best idea, Mam—and all for what, a photograph?'

Liam suddenly appears inside the telephone box beside her, sporting the navy blazer and chinos he wore for Connie's birthday. There isn't a speck of dirt on his clothes or a scratch on his handsome face.

'Why didn't you tell me you got out early?' he asks. 'I had to find out from the papers!'

'I didn't want to interrupt your training. Where are you today? Portugal, I presume?'

'You're changing the subject. I thought you'd jump at the chance to leave this country and those bloody reporters. Like Mary Elizabeth and Gerry had the sense to do. Don't you want sunshine? I've found the perfect house for us. One thing's for sure, it's a step up from that kip of a guesthouse in Dublin, with fellas pissing all over the carpets. You should, at least, have stayed in my apartment. Why didn't you?'

Lounging in a penthouse suite in Blackrock or sunning herself on a golden beach in the Algarve was laughable to Connie. 'Not right now.'

'Mam, I need you.'

'I need you, too, but …'

Liam sighs. 'Well, if you don't come to me, I'll return to Ireland. Mam, there's no way of sugarcoating it, but you are Public Enemy Number One. Do you realise how dangerous it is for you outside of prison? I'm not allowing you to roam about this village or the streets of Dublin alone.'

'But you are here.'

'I need to be *really* here—not just a figment of your imagination.'

'A figment of my imagination is more than enough for now. So long as you're in my heart and mind, I'll get by.'

'But Mam—'

'That's enough now, Liam.'

'If you say so. By the way, are you sure the bus still comes through the village?'

'Why wouldn't it?' Connie hears drilling nearby and remembers what the driver explained earlier that morning. 'The roadworks, of course.'

'And now you've missed the eleven o'clock bus, so you'll have to wait another two hours for the next one. Just promise me you'll keep out of sight.'

As Connie prepares to flee the square, she spots a figure emerging from the café's kitchen: Andy, Jess' uncle.

'I'm going on my break,' he tells the server, opening the door. 'If anybody else wants food, they'll have to wait.'

Ignoring the drizzle of rain, Andy sits on the window ledge and chances a cigarette.

'Mam, don't move,' Liam warns, 'otherwise, he's going to see you.' But it's too late.

'What the hell are *you* doing here?' Andy roars when he spots Connie in the telephone box. He flings his cigarette to the ground, pulls the door open and drags her into the café.

'I'm sorry. I'm so sorry.'

'Hey, what's going on?' the server cries, racing from behind the counter and standing in between them. Not that a human barrier will deter Andy. He hurls the remains of the customer's breakfast towards Connie, its contents splattering over her face, coat and handbag. The plate barely misses her head and smashes against the painting of the lighthouse instead.

'If it wasn't for the fact that my back is in ribbons, I'd throw you through the wall!'

'I'm sorry,' Connie repeats. 'Tell Breege that I'm sorry.'

'My sister doesn't care what you've to say. It's hardly going to bring anyone back. Eighteen months instead of twenty-eight. Even twenty-eight years isn't enough for you—you should have been given the lethal injection! Although, with everything you've been taking over the years, you'd probably be immune to injections at this stage.'

He pushes her backwards, knocking tables and chairs as they go.

'You pulled the wool over everyone's eyes, I'll give you that, Connie Maguire. And to think, we were all convinced that you were sweet and funny, making corny jokes and not hurting a fly. How wrong were we? Jess adored the bones of you, and you repay her by becoming her bloody killer!'

Covered in scrambled eggs and beans, Connie finally escapes the café and races across the square, ignoring the sudden downpour. The server holds Andy back at the door. Shop owners and their customers spill onto the picture-perfect streets, anxious to understand the commotion.

CHAPTER EIGHT

THEN, SATURDAY AFTERNOON

CONNIE AND JESS sat in the back garden at one of the many tables borrowed from Gerry's café. For now, all the food remained indoors, much to the chagrin of a cluster of hungry starlings who spent the past five minutes hoping for scraps. A light breeze eventually encouraged them to find their fortunes elsewhere.

Bunting, balloons, inflatable flamingos, piñatas, paper lanterns and strings of fairy lights transformed Connie's back garden into something straight out of the social pages of a glossy magazine. There was even a booth where guests could dress up in sombreros and ponchos and have their photos taken. A girlfriend of Liam's teammate on the Leinster squad had organised most of the flourishes, ignoring Connie's instructions to keep everything simple.

Gerry and his husband were helping Liam make a bowl of sangria in the kitchen, using generous measures of red wine and brandy.

'*Chicas*, how about a little tipple to get us in the mood before the guests arrive?' Mary Elizabeth suggested, strutting out of the kitchen and placing two flutes overflowing with cava beside Jess' makeup bag. Wearing a gold sequinned mini-dress and laurel wreath headpiece, Mary Elizabeth had come dressed to party. 'Or would the birthday girl prefer a beer?'

Connie had previously avoided drinks like cava and prosecco and, especially, champagne. The only time she had sampled bubbles was at a wedding in Athlone, but she battled a headache for two days and vowed never to touch them again. A former counsellor suggested her aversion to these drinks stemmed from a feeling of being 'unworthy of pampering'. Connie now readily accepted the glass and enjoyed a mouthful.

New beginnings.

Mary Elizabeth returned towards the house. 'I'm going to spend a penny, but, Jess, you might give the back of my hair a little seeing-to afterwards?'

'A little bird tells me you're bringing someone to the barbecue later,' Jess teased, her energy as effervescent as the drinks on the table. 'We'll make sure he's weak at the knees!'

'It'll be me who's weak at the knees if I don't go easy on the cava because it's going straight through me! Won't be a minute, ladies.'

Jess, who'd recently completed a beauty course, was more than happy to offer her services to the two women who'd shown her more love over the past couple of years than her own mother had throughout her entire life. Though only twenty-one, Jess possessed maturity beyond her years, a result of having to act like an adult since she was a child.

'An old but beautiful head,' Connie had always clarified, following Jess' mock protestations about being called old. And she really was beautiful. Aside from her lithesome physique and tanned skin, perfectly showcased today in a teal, one-shoulder jumpsuit, her hazel eyes were what photographers killed for.

After some deliberation, Jess chose red nail varnish to contrast with the birthday girl's yellow maxi dress. 'I hope you like what I've picked—you can never go wrong with the classic colours.'

Connie, now leaning back on the chair, smiled. 'I've every faith in you, my love.'

The medication was taking effect. She took another sip, determined that it would be a day of celebration, regardless of whatever obstacles emerged. If only she had naturally claimed this confidence and positivity.

'You've lovely hands, do you know that?' Jess praised. 'That means you're curious—so I'm told, anyway. I think that's a good description of you.'

If it weren't for the tablet, Connie would probably have argued that she was far from curious and that her fingers were short and stubby.

'When you're repeatedly told you're worthless, it's easy to believe it,' that same counsellor had suggested.

For now, the tablet had silenced Connie's self-critical demons. 'Thank you, Jess. That's a lovely thing to say.'

The women had clicked right away. When Jess tentatively revealed fragments of her fractured relationship with Breege, Connie confided that she knew what it was like growing up with an abusive parent. Jess joked it was the reason she'd pursued a career in makeup—'I already have a lifetime of experience covering up the emotional scars.'

Unlike Connie's childhood, there had been no name-calling. Instead, Jess spoke about her mother's destructive alcoholism and violent outbursts, along with the strange men constantly being brought back to the house at ungodly hours. And, most shockingly, the OnlyFans videos Breege once filmed in her bedroom. Even after all that, Jess told Connie that she still loved her mother and hoped against hope a miracle would occur. That, somehow, she'd get her life in order.

'Connie, do you believe in change?' Jess asked, tackling another nail. 'Or what's that expression about leopards and spots?'

'Or leading a horse to water but being unable to force it to drink?' Connie was familiar with this phrase, as Mary Elizabeth often said it to her during her own recovery. 'I suppose clichés are used because they're often true, making it frustrating when you want to help someone. In your case …'

'My mam.'

'Your mam, yes. I think people must want to change, but they also need the tools and support system to do it.'

Without the tough love shown to her by her son and best friend over the years, Connie dreaded thinking about where she would have ended up. Today's transgression was just a one-off to feel less overwhelmed by the day. She looked at Jess, her pretty face furrowed in concentration.

'Your mam is very lucky to have you.'

'She has recently launched an online store,' Jess revealed. 'Maybe that will give her a focus. Feel proud, you know? Anyway, I doubt things can get much worse. I'd to do her makeup this morning because she'd an accident pole-dancing on a lamppost in front of The Steeples the other night.'

'It's important to stay positive, isn't it?' Connie couldn't believe how effortlessly her hypocrisy was revealing itself.

'If only every mam was as amazing as you!'

This compliment made Connie recoil, leading her to knock over the nail polish. She caught it just before it fell to the ground.

'That's kind of you to say, Jess, but we're all flawed in one way or another—some of us are better at hiding it than others.'

She took another sip, a moment to decide what to say next. 'Often, we're trying to undo the damage done to us by our parents and more than likely, so were they. One of my books suggests we're the reluctant inheritors of the generations that have come before us. I like that expression, "the reluctant inheritors". The abuse keeps getting passed on until someone is strong enough to say "stop". It takes courage to break those vicious cycles, but I've every faith you'll do exactly that.'

'Have you? Broken those vicious cycles, I mean. With your mother.'

'It's a strange thing, Jess: even though she's dead, the debris remains, as my former counsellor would tell you. But I'm getting better at letting go. I'm afraid I'm not there yet because it doesn't happen overnight, but I'm improving.'

'Well,' Jess said after blowing on the finished nails, 'with you as a role model, I'm going to work on it, too.'

Shame undermined the tablet's golden glow, so Connie reached for her cava and took another gulp.

CHAPTER NINE
NOW

THE WOOD DOMINATING the south of the village has always been Connie's favourite place. Over the years, she spent hours traipsing along the abandoned canal, a haven for wildlife like herons, water hens, otters and badgers. She regularly retreated here while battling moments of temptation or during spells of feeling worthless and lonely. Or if she wanted to scream into the ether following fights with her mother. Few knew about it, outside of the locals, meaning it remained unspoiled and, much to Connie's advantage this morning, free from people.

There are two agonising hours to pass before the Dublin-bound bus returns. She leans against a tree and closes her eyes, attempting to centre herself following a morning fraught with emotion and anxiety. It was the confirmation she dreaded receiving: her village would never again be her home. Immediately after the crash, Teddy warned her this would happen. How could it be any other way? But experiencing that contempt first-hand today made her want to vomit.

Where her belongings have ended up is anyone's guess. The best-case scenario is that her former landlord has stored them, but she wouldn't be surprised if Breege and Andy had played a part in their disappearance. During the party, Liam had caught Breege swiping some presents gifted to him by companies eager for shout-outs across his popular social media pages.

'I was going to sell them on my new website,' she had claimed when caught in the act.

Rather than selling them, Connie imagines Breege setting fire to her possessions and memories. She is welcome to do that. The photograph is the only item she needs from her former life, wherever it may be.

'I'm proud of you, Mam.'

Liam leans against the tree that once flung his younger self from its branches, a nasty accident resulting in ten stitches under his chin.

'Proud? Why? For upsetting Andy?'

'No, I'm still furious about you being here. All for what, a photograph in a fancy frame? And, while I'm complaining, the council should organise more buses—one every two hours is ridiculous. But no, I'm proud you haven't gone near the pharmacy.'

'Those days are in the past.'

Unlike his mother, Liam is bone dry and tanned.

'I imagine the weather in Portugal is a far cry from what we're experiencing here today.'

'I must send you a postcard, Mam. I'll arrange something with the concierge.'

'Where will you send it?'

'I can't believe our bloody landlord brought in new tenants without consulting me. If I were here, *really here*, I'd throttle him.'

'I know you would.' And Connie means it. As much as she adores her only child, Liam's weakness has always been his temper, especially during those hormone-fuelled teenage years. He once punched a hole in the bathroom door when his so-called father had, for the umpteenth time, forgotten his birthday. That was one reason Connie had readily encouraged his interest in rugby; along with the many role models he gained, the sport allowed him to channel his frustrations constructively. His relationship with Jess had been another turning point in overcoming his demons. The young lovebirds had bonded over their shared experiences. Along with having absent fathers, both their mothers battled addictions. Not that Liam, as far as she knew, shared much about Connie's situation with anyone outside the family other than Mary Elizabeth.

'You must be grateful to be released ten months early,' he now says.

'There's very little I'm grateful for at the minute.'

'You see, that's the sort of talk that has me worried sick about you! No wonder I can barely kick a ball straight this week. You think you're doing me a favour by not interrupting my training, but I'm even more distracted not knowing where or how you are.'

'I'm fine.'

'Of course you're fine, Mam,' he shoots back. 'You're in the middle of the wood, soaking wet, with beans and scrambled eggs in your hair. Let me organise something for you over here, even some temporary work if you want to keep busy. Not that we need money—it's disgusting, but the sponsors say my stock has soared because everyone feels sorry for me after the crash. What I'm saying is you don't have to do this alone. I want to take care of you. And, selfishly, I want you to take care of me, too. I miss Jess so much. I miss you both.'

'I'll call you later today, I promise. I hope you're eating.'

'More than you are clearly. Not very nice of Andy to waste good food like that. I hope the customer didn't leave that thug a tip.'

'It was my fault, thinking I'd be hidden in the telephone box. Why didn't I remember the bus wasn't going through the village? I've hurt him all over again.'

'He was hardly a saint to Jess when she was alive. They were a bunch of animals, that family. And still are, clearly.'

A siren ringing in the distance distracts her. She imagines the police car is driven by Teddy, the man who vowed 'never, ever' to speak to her again mere hours after gifting her a family heirloom, his grandmother's beautiful necklace. She last saw him in the courthouse, paler than ever. The judge praised him for the precision and honesty of his testimony against the woman he had loved since primary school.

'Today is especially difficult for you, given your lifelong friendship,' the judge had commented. 'But the defendant's negligent driving has resulted in the tragic loss of life. I'm relieved that justice has been your priority today, Sergeant.'

'Hey!' a voice, a real one, bellows from a garden. 'What are you doing?'

Connie immediately realises the voice belongs to Mandy Waldron, a villager obsessed with hoarding. Teddy would regularly refer to her stash as a 'deathtrap'. Everything she acquired was scattered in bags and boxes in her back garden, and if anyone dared touch them, including members of the Gardaí, Mandy would whip them with her stick.

'I'm just chatting to my son,' Connie replies, approaching her through the scrub.

Mandy, who was usually the recipient of other people's stares, throws her a look of suspicion, straightens her stooped back and scans the area. 'Where is he?'

But Liam has disappeared.

'He better not be rooting through my things.' Mandy inspects her garden; thankfully, everything seems in order. A large dog stands beside, ready to offer protection.

'Hey, you've managed to get something in your hair,' Mandy says to Connie through fits of laughter. 'Beans, is it? I love beans, although I'd never think to put them in my hair.'

'I had an accident with my breakfast earlier. I'm a bit clumsy today.'

'Well, I've nothing to offer you, sorry. I gave my bread to the birds, but they seem to be staying home today, out of the rain. They've eaten nothing. A waste. Like your lovely beans. Maybe I like food too much—look at the belly on me!' She pulls up her multiple layers of clothing to reveal a healthy, rotund stomach. 'My sister calls me "pudgy"! Isn't she a brat? Her goldfish died, so I'll say nothing, but she wouldn't want to keep it up. "Pudgy"! Funny word.'

While retrieving the remaining food from her hair, Connie notices a ceramic vase in a trolley in Mandy's garden, a prize she won in the Christmas raffle fifteen years earlier. Beside it is a flowerpot, similar to the one an enraged Liam smashed during the party. She notices many of her possessions stacked high at the back of the trolley: books, cutlery, cushions and yoga mats. And between them sits something that she has desperately wanted to reclaim all morning: the framed photograph.

'I don't believe it,' she whispers. 'Mandy, where did you get these things?'

'They're my things!'

'Yes,' Connie concedes, not wanting to cause upset, 'they're yours, but where did you get them?'

'In the skip beside the weir,' Mandy reluctantly informs her, guarding her spoils. 'I think you should leave. People are always trying to take my things.'

'Can I ask you one favour before I go?'

Mandy considers the request for a moment. 'A little one.'

'Do you see that photograph in the crystal frame? Do you recognise the woman standing beside the boy in the rugby jersey?'

Curious, Mandy holds it to her face, then shrugs.

'Do you think she looks like me?'

Mandy slowly traces her finger over the two figures. 'This person seems happier. And fatter—"pudgier", as herself would say. Are you sisters?'

'No, that's me. Many, many years ago. With my son.'

'Wait. Does he play rugby?' Mandy asks, staring at Connie and then at the photograph, a glimmer of recognition crossing her face. 'I know them, don't I? A terrible accident. Near Kavanagh's barn. The girl died, didn't she? She was beautiful. Could have been a film star like Joan Crawford or Ava Gardner.'

Connie nods.

'I met her only hours before.'

'Did you?' Connie's mind flashes back to Jess' message, saying she was here but would return soon.

'She was trying to calm him down,' Mandy continues, pointing at the photo. 'He was angry—his face was red and scrunched like it was about to burst. She stopped to say hello and petted Daisy.'

'Did she?'

'Nobody goes near Daisy. The girl wasn't scared, though. Himself calmed down too soon after. She was a good influence, I'd say.'

'The best.'

Mandy hands the photo to Connie. 'Here. But you're not getting anything else.'

'This is all I need.'

CHAPTER TEN
THEN, SATURDAY AFTERNOON

'I HOPE EVERYBODY has covered themselves in sun cream!'

Mary Elizabeth passed around bottles of Nivea to the fifty-odd guests. The sun had appeared, meaning many people scattered across the patio and garden now resembled the tomatoes that coloured Connie's much-praised salads.

'Sun cream, everyone!' Mary Elizabeth repeated. 'No one wants to be making appointments with the dermatologist on Monday to get new lesions checked, do they?'

Connie's gregarious best friend was famed for her contributions to every party she attended, so long as her latest squeeze didn't distract her. Today, he was an accountant named Rory and judging by his unwillingness to converse with words other than 'yes' or 'no', Connie doubted that he'd still be in her life by the time the birthday candles were extinguished.

'Your friend is joining us, right?' Connie overheard Mary Elizabeth ask Rory. 'What did you say his name was?'

'Bosco.'

'Like the children's show?'

'It's common in Donegal.'

'That's where he's from, is it?'

'Yes.'

'But he works in Navan?'

'Yes.'

'And he'll be here later?'

'Yes.'

'And he's a good lad, is he?'

'Yes.'

'Jesus, Rory, I hope you're better with numbers than words. You should think of writing a book one day as you've clearly the gift of the gab.'

Connie smiled, unsure if Mary Elizabeth or Rory deserved her pity. Or this Bosco person, whoever he was. She caught her breath by the back door, delighted that everything was running smoothly and her son's efforts with the barbecue were nothing short of triumphant. She savoured the atmosphere. Everyone she loved most was here, including her father and his best friends, Kenny and Heather, the closest people she had to an uncle and aunt. Nick and Breege had yet to arrive.

'I thought your talents were on the pitch rather than in the kitchen,' Mary Elizabeth quipped as she approached Liam at the barbecue. 'If we'd known that you were so handy around a rasher and sausage, your mammy could have asked you to help with the dinners more often. Or Gerry could have given you a job over in the café.'

'It's a good thing that I kept my secret talents to myself,' Liam replied, taking a large bite of a burger. Over the past hour, guests had handed him a jumble of drinks and the day was still young, so he desperately needed sustenance. Otherwise, it would be game over before the evening Angelus.

'Well, I mightn't stand to benefit from these revelations,' Connie said. 'But Jess, I hope you're going to force this son of mine to throw on an apron now and then!'

'What about my training?'

'Don't worry, I'll make sure this fella's feet will be kept firmly on the ground,' Jess teased. 'By the way, it's great to see you so relaxed, Connie. You must have nerves of steel because I was a disaster at my twenty-first. I don't know how often I powdered my face to hide the blushing.'

'A long soak in the tub always works wonders for me.'

'I hope nobody confuses foot cream for sun cream today,' Kenny interjected from his chair, 'unlike someone did a few years ago.'

As Liam explained his childhood mistake to Jess, which resulted not only in sunburn to the face but a nasty allergic reaction that made him temporarily blind, Connie approached her ghostlike father, sitting slumped beside Kenny. 'Dad, would you like more food?'

With every passing day, his dementia slowly worsened. Compounding matters, he had also picked up a stomach bug recently. Once, his height and broad frame commanded attention everywhere he went; now, the seventy-eight-year-old was unrecognisable from his former self with his hunched back and thin limbs. If he were on the home stretch, Connie's only comfort would be that he was well looked after in the nursing home. His new carer briefly appeared earlier in the afternoon. He seemed kind and capable. And, according to Mary Elizabeth, he was also 'ridiculously handsome'.

'Imelda,' her father whispered to her—he'd developed a habit of calling everyone by that name—'this is a lovely get-together. Did you receive my present? It's under the elderberry bush.'

'I did, Dad, and I loved it.' He was referring to the pair of roller skates he'd bought for her twelfth birthday, a present she'd longed for since Mary Elizabeth had received a pair from an aunt in Boston that summer. 'I can't wait to try them out. Thank you. I hope you'll come and watch me skate.'

'I won't be able to, Imelda. I'm busy sailing on a boat. But it's too foggy. I can't even see the callows on either side of me.'

'Is that right, Dad?'

'Sadly, there's nothing right about it, Imelda. I'll have no choice but to start the engine of the propeller plane instead and fly over it.'

'Sounds exciting but dangerous. I hope you won't get hurt.'

Travelling was now a constant theme in her father's ramblings, surprising, considering he was a home bird who barely stepped foot on a plane his entire life, not even to visit his in-laws in Nuremberg.

'Where are the eggs? I've come all this way to the farm, and I'd like an egg, please. Fried.'

'Let me see if I can rustle up some for you now, Captain. I'll get your grandson—the two-legged mouse—on the case.'

That was her father's nickname for Liam because, growing up, the youngster would regularly swipe biscuits from the tin when nobody was looking, meaning there was rarely anything to offer visitors besides bread.

'A mouse? I couldn't stomach a mouse, even if it had only two legs. Just an egg, Imelda. Fried. I'll wait here. Unless the tide goes out. Mice with only two legs—what's the world coming to?'

'I understand. Kenny, will you do me a favour? Kenny?'

Her father's best friend, who Connie always thought resembled Santa Claus, struggled with hearing, so she leaned closer to him. 'Kenny, could you move the umbrella so that Dad's arm is under it?'

'Sorry, yes.'

'Thank you. By the way, I'm so happy you two are here.'

'Wild horses couldn't keep us away,' Heather replied. She was always immaculately turned out, and today was no different. Channelling Jackie O, she wore a blue tweed jacket and matching skirt, but her effortless style couldn't detract from her frailty. Along with a chronic lung condition, she was booked in for a hip operation before Christmas. Cooking had been central to every visit to their home by the bog, and Heather had taught Connie a cornucopia of recipes over the years. Now, the woman could barely touch the food in front of her.

'Reaching old bones is certainly a privilege,' Connie's former neighbour had once mused, 'but it's not without its disadvantages.' Looking at the trio in front of her, she was reminded of the accuracy of this observation.

'I must say, it's lovely to see you so relaxed,' Heather praised. 'That yoga has transformed you!'

'I'd be lost without it. How's Prince, by the way?' Connie asked, quickly changing the subject. 'Still biting you?'

'I swear, that cat must have been a vampire in a past life!'

After asking Liam to fry some eggs for his grandfather, Connie returned to the kitchen, dancelike, to prepare the desserts.

'What will you do now that he's moving out for good?' Mary Elizabeth quizzed, helping her with the fridge door. 'You need to take a leaf out of my book and start dating! I know one person who'll be at the top of that queue.'

'Did I show you his gorgeous present?'

'About twenty times! And I don't blame you. I knew Teddy had good taste in women, but I didn't realise it extended to jewellery. It's only gorgeous. I should start paying him more attention. My social calendar is jam-packed in the run-up to Christmas, so I could do with his granny's bling to liven up my new outfits.'

'Can I tell you a secret?' Connie whispered as she retrieved a tub of ice cream from the freezer. 'I talk to him when he's not here.'

'Who? Teddy?'

Connie laughed. 'Liam. It's silly, I know. I started when he joined the Leinster team. I was, you know …'

'Lonely?'

'Maybe lonely. But I think it's more that I was doubting myself and my decisions. When your mother tells you daily that you're wrong, you believe it. Unlike me, Liam has grown to be so assertive and rational. That's why he's so good at what he does.'

'That sort of makes sense.'

'If I've got a decision to make, I ask myself: what would Liam do? Not always, but sometimes. I have conversations with him like an imaginary friend. Or a less-expensive counsellor. The real Liam is constantly catching me talking to the imaginary Liam!'

If only Connie had talked to her imaginary son earlier in the bedroom, 'Liam' might have steered her from falling back into old ways.

'The first sign of madness,' Mary Elizabeth said. 'Does he slag you about these chats, then? He should.'

'He thinks it's sweet, but now I worry he feels guilty about leaving me alone. He was even worried about telling me the news that he'd made the team.'

'Well, more reason for you to start dating again, you loony! Which reminds me, you know how we all loved to watch *Bosco*, well …'

But Connie never discovered why Mary Elizabeth was bringing the once-popular, red-headed puppet into the conversation because her attention drifted outside, thanks to the party's latest arrival.

'Hey, stranger,' Nick said, walking into the kitchen, his voice as smooth as the ice cream melting in Connie's hand. 'It's been a while.'

CHAPTER ELEVEN

NOW

CONNIE WALKS GINGERLY along the canal towpath towards the correct bus stop, with Liam keeping her company. After that incident with Andy in the café, she knows Breege is now hunting for her prey. 'Liam' and their photo, hidden in her handbag, calm her. After crossing a lock, she stops and stares at the silhouettes of tombstones and a church steeple in the distance: it is the old graveyard where her parents are buried.

'Please, don't even think about it, Mam.'

Contradictory instructions infiltrate her mind: 'Go', 'Don't go'. She needs to say goodbye to her father, and seeing as this will probably be her last time in the village, she ignores Liam's advice and her better judgement and rushes along the side of the field before hiding behind the wall, allowing a former neighbour to finish tending a grave.

Walking past the ivy-covered church ruins moments later, Connie is thankful that her parents are buried here amongst friends and not in the newer, often-flooded cemetery near Drogheda, where Jess was laid to rest. She shudders at the thought of her under the damp soil.

Apart from a couple of anniversaries and the occasional blessings of the graves, Connie rarely visited her mother here following her funeral.

'Isn't it shocking that you haven't shed a few tears for your poor, dead mother—the least you could have done was say a Prayer of the Faithful during the mass,' a local farmer had remarked while 'paying his condolences' to Connie, graveside. But she couldn't have been expected to mourn the tyrant. When told that the sixty-year-old had succumbed to a heart attack in Navan Shopping Centre, she thought it strange, convinced that her mother hadn't ever been equipped with that particular organ. No, there had been no tears during the funeral and burial.

Nor was it an occasion for celebration, either. Connie had once read that there was a strange beauty in grief because it was pure and uncomplicated: you're sad because someone you love is no longer here. That day, Connie realised the flaws and over-simplicity of that statement. Grief *was* complicated and chaotic and oppressive. How do you mourn someone nature tells you to love, but reality demands that you avoid for self-survival? While she had prided herself on having the strength to remove the toxic woman from her life, it always saddened Connie that she had to make such a drastic move in the first place. If she had received the nurturing of a loving mother, someone who hadn't blamed her for 'destroying' her womb and being unable to conceive more children, things might have turned out differently for Connie. She wouldn't have become so dependent on tablets, at least. Her counsellor had repeatedly encouraged her to forgive and release the grip the woman still had on her, even in death.

'Why is the onus of forgiveness always on me?' Connie shot back during their first session. 'If my mother were sitting here and not me, she'd laugh at you and demand a full refund. She always said that apologies and forgiveness were only for the weak. Unless it was apologising to God for our dirty sins.'

Standing in front of the grave today, Connie is surprised to see it partially covered with fresh flowers fifteen months after her father's death. Initially, she thinks it was Liam before reasoning that her father had once been a popular plumber in the community. Connie is glad that the fall-out from that night hasn't tarnished his reputation. Not for the first time, she wonders what his funeral was like. Did many mourners pay their respects? Was there music, singing or poetry? And, unlike her mother's funeral, were there tears? Getting answers to all those questions would have been easy because Liam started telling her about the day once during a visit. But Connie wanted to avoid learning about her former life, whether it was Breege's grief or her father's send-off.

'You can tell me again,' she had said without ever following it up.

When she was a child, her father would play his banjo at bedtime and sing her to sleep with his low, gravelly voice—a tradition he continued with Liam. Connie hoped someone sang to him during his funeral when it was his turn to sleep for the final time.

Seeing his name carved on the black marble headstone below her mother's feels strange. Her parents reunited. At least they can't fight now, although Connie can still hear her mother's piercing German accent from beyond the grave.

'I told you that daughter of yours would amount to nothing!' she can imagine her mother grouse. 'Any fat *schlampe* who spent half of her days down alleyways with boys would always end up in prison!'

Connie often joked to Mary Elizabeth that she wished she'd been half as promiscuous as her mother had made out. Apart from awkward kisses with blind dates, she had only been truly intimate with Nick. But her mother never had any interest in facts.

Realising her mind is wandering into dark and dangerous places, she heads towards the bus stop but halts. Nearly every moment since her father's death, Connie has wanted to thank him for loving her. For protecting her.

It's too late now.

As she nears the exit, the voices in her head are replaced by a different, more distressing sound: the furious clicking of cameras.

'Over here, Connie!' one of three photographers shouts, emerging from behind the church.

'Will you visit Jess' next?' another interrupts. 'What does Liam think of you being here? Didn't he want to come back to Ireland ahead of your release? To be by your side?'

They form a triangle behind her and close in. Liam had predicted that they would pre-empt her every move, then make the cruellest comments imaginable to get a reaction from her—the 'money shot', as he'd described it.

'Has Liam invited you to join him in the Algarve? Are you still taking tablets? And drinking? Are you drunk right now?'

'Are you looking forward to the World Cup? What do you think Ireland's chances are? Have you been following their progress from prison?'

'How will Liam fare after everything that's happened?'

Connie quickens her pace and grips the photo in her handbag while repeating Liam's advice to ignore them. She battles the urge to roar back at them because that's what they want. Once reporters and photographers set their sights on a target, they become relentless and vicious. Andy, or one of the other villagers, probably posted something on social media earlier, maybe a video of her fleeing the café, beans dripping down her face. She knows they have raced here from Dublin, Belfast or God-knows-where and are now determined to make their trip here worthwhile.

'Come on, Connie! We thought you'd be itching to chat after being locked up in Mountjoy. Tell us: does Liam hate you for killing the love of his life?'

Connie spies a rock sitting on the wall, but before she can contemplate hurling it at them, Teddy and his colleague, Jack, jump out of a police car.

'What do you think you're doing, you gurriers? I thought I told you to leave the village,' Teddy shouts, storming past Connie and forcing the photographers out of the graveyard. A lawnmower springs to life in a nearby garden, drowning out the photographers' protestations about having rights. Connie continues out of the village, passing the smiling lion mascot, his thumbs pointing upwards.

CHAPTER TWELVE
THEN, SATURDAY AFTERNOON

CONNIE SAT NEXT to Nick on the front garden wall, the hot stone uncomfortable under her legs. The additional tablet she had just swallowed had yet to take effect. They were away from the other guests, including his stunning and ever-so-young girlfriend, Izzy, although Connie knew they were staring at them from the living room. Even though dark circles had formed under Nick's eyes, and the lines across his forehead suggested his overindulgences extended beyond his teenage years, his Hollywood looks hadn't entirely abandoned him. And when he smiled, it was almost as if she were looking at Liam.

Along with white trainers and flashy jewellery, Nick wore a jungle-patterned, sleeveless shirt and skinny grey jeans, an ensemble that might have been more flattering on someone half his age. Connie suspected that this was a man ill-prepared to embrace his vintage. Hoping to conceal the effect he continued to hold over her, Connie distracted herself by sipping a large glass of chardonnay.

'He's a great lad,' Nick eventually said, his overfamiliarity roiling Connie. 'I was a good rugby player myself, you know, Con. Back in the day. He takes after me, I'd say. But credit where credit's due, you didn't do a bad job. Well done.'

Well done?

He didn't have a clue about the difficulties of being a single parent: constantly worrying whether Liam was safe, struggling for money and sacrificing her social life, not to mention abandoning her dream of being a nurse. The man knew nothing of those countless nights when their son had cried for hours on end. Or battled croup. Or when he sat in silence after some kid at school teased him for not having a dad.

'Thank you,' she replied, determined not to let herself down. 'Are you working these days?'

He threw her the same contemptuous look that had crossed his face when Connie announced the pregnancy twenty-four years earlier. 'As opposed to what, kicking stones? Of course I work. I run a private club in Dublin for VIPs.'

'Sounds lovely.'

'It wouldn't be your style, Connie,' he interrupted, swatting a midge. 'Speaking of style, now that Liam has made the Ireland team, he won't live in this dump for much longer, huh?'

Connie wasn't sure if he was referring to her home or the village—either way, she ignored the comments and allowed her silence to speak for her.

'Why he didn't move out years ago is beyond me,' Nick continued. 'He probably felt guilty leaving you all alone. I take it you didn't meet anyone.'

Connie knew he was uninterested in hearing the response and imagined the lull in the conversation was proving too much for him. She shook her head.

'I suppose it's difficult for a single mother. It would probably be a turnoff for most fellas.'

Breathe and release, Connie. Breathe and release.

'How about you, Nick? Did you meet someone?'

'Didn't you just say hello to her?'

'Oh, yes, of course, Izzy,' Connie stammered. The familiar note of irritation in his voice rattled her.

'Asking whether we've children would have been a better question. And no, I've no children.'

'Apart from Liam.'

'Apart from Liam. By the way,' he said aggressively, sitting upright. 'Why did you choose the name Liam? It's a bit bland.'

Connie nearly smashed her glass across his head. But that would be a waste of drink.

'And I thought it was usual for the kid to get the father's surname, no? The number of people who don't believe he's my son, even though he obviously gets his good looks from me. And I know my parents are still furious about him being a Maguire. By the way, would it have hurt you to invite them here today? After all, they are his grandparents and basically paid for his entire upbringing. It's only good manners, really.'

'All right, Nick, there's no need to have a fit.'

His face suddenly contorted. 'What did you say? That's a low blow, even for you, Connie.'

'What?'

'Bringing up my epilepsy. You haven't changed your ways.'

Connie muttered an apology but stopped short of correcting his misinterpretation of her comment; what was the point?

'Liam Maguire—sounds like some bloody farmer's son,' he continued. 'He'll not pull too many ladies with a sheep-shagging name like that.'

'He has a girlfriend, Jess—haven't you met her?'

Nick scoffed. 'I'll give it another week if she's lucky. The girl's cute, though, so *she*, at least, won't be long on the shelf.'

He threw her a patronising, poor-you glance. Connie didn't have time to reply as Kenny and Heather, arms linked, emerged from the cottage.

'We were looking for you to say goodbye,' Kenny said, kissing her. 'We had a wonderful afternoon, didn't we, Heather?'

'We certainly did. Your father is in his element, and he's currently telling Mary Elizabeth all about JFK. And devouring fried eggs!'

'Well, it made my day having you two here.'

'Aren't you going to introduce us, Connie?' Nick interrupted, huffy from being ignored. He offered Kenny his hand. 'I'm—'

'We know who you are,' Kenny cut in, 'but I don't want to ruin the day for Connie and Liam—otherwise, I'd be wiping that stupid grin from your face. Come on, Heather, we'd better go. We don't want to be held up in traffic or face assault charges.'

After Kenny put Nick in his place, Connie decided that, for once, she wouldn't play Ms Nice and indulge in any further small talk. She would sit in stony silence. As Kenny and Heather disappeared down the road, she watched Nick's arrogance abandon him; it was his turn to fidget and look around.

'You take good care of your gardens. It must be difficult for your landlord to get insurance on a thatched cottage, though.'

Connie looked straight ahead.

'Do you go to The Steeples much?'

No response.

'God, Connie, do you have to make this so difficult? You're as dull now as you were back in school. Liam must have inherited his personality from me,' Nick continued, retrieving a packet of cigarettes from his pocket. However, without the assistance of any lighter, he had finally managed to spark a reaction in Connie. She stood up.

'There's absolutely nothing similar about you and Liam! My son is a gentleman with the biggest heart imaginable.'

'You sound like a granny—zip it, will you?'

'He's nothing like you. You? You?' she stuttered, momentarily losing her train of thought. 'You are a leech, a parasite—sponging off anyone and everyone! He might not see through your schtick today or tomorrow, but he will. Eventually. Like everyone always does! And don't ever tell me to "zip it" in my own house!'

After a brief pause, Nick laughed and began slowly clapping his hands.

'How long have you been rehearsing that one? Not bad, I must say. I particularly liked the word "schtick". You don't hear it used that often these days. So, "Connie with the Ronnie",' he hissed, holding his middle finger in front of him, 'why don't you *schtick* this—'

'And why don't you *schtick* some of the prawns into your gob before leaving,' she cut in. 'Slippery little bastards, aren't they? Just like you!'

She knew it wasn't a comeback worthy of awards or acclaim, but for Connie Maguire, it was a moment of triumph. She hadn't once challenged Nick in her entire life.

New beginnings, she reminded herself.

With impeccable timing, Breege, Andy and several friends sped down the lane in a white van.

'Time to get this party started!' Breege roared, draping herself across the opened window. After taking a long swig from a vodka bottle, she attempted to place a pink cowboy hat over her short, dark hair, eventually succeeding. 'Am I right, Connie?'

'Time to get this party started!' Connie echoed, raising her now empty glass.

Admitting defeat, Nick walked away, spitting, 'Tell Izzy I'll wait for her in the car.'

Feeling invincible, the birthday girl ushered her new guests, along with their keg, into the back garden.

* * *

'Why did she say that? I mean, I'd expect one of those "Karens" who complain about everything to leave me a bad review, but this one is my first cousin, you know?'

Leaning against the kitchen sink, Connie rubbed Breege's arm. She'd recently launched an online fashion boutique selling second-hand, upcycled clothing. From her description, it was hard to imagine the enterprise threatening eBay or Etsy, but Connie was impressed by Breege's desire for a second chance in life. However, familial support for her efforts was wanting.

'Blood is thicker and all that,' the budding entrepreneur added. 'Speaking of water.'

She reached past Connie and filled a plastic cup from the tap, only partially succeeding in hitting her target.

'I've one or two in me now, Connie,' she continued, the water proving to be as unhelpful as her cousin if the sudden deterioration in her speech was anything to go by, 'and the last thing you want to be doing on your special day is listening to me. But you know I've had my difficulties—God knows, I still have my difficulties—but I'm trying. I am. Honest to God I am.'

'You're playing a blinder. I know Jess is proud of you.'

'Is she?'

'Of course she is. We all are. It was a rotten thing for your cousin to do. Let me tell you, if she ever comes to this village, I'll give her a good talking to!'

Given how well she stuck up for herself with Nick, Connie believed anything was now possible.

'You do that, Connie, although she'll probably laugh in your face—you're hardly G.I. Jane. Actually, you are, come to think of it. And maybe that's where you're going wrong. You might want to think about binning those combats if you want to get a fella. What you have on you today is gorgeous, though.'

'Thank you, Breege—that's high praise, seeing as you're a fashionista.'

'Tell that to my cousin. I appreciate the support, though. And this coleslaw—it's absolutely delicious.'

'Made it myself only this—'

'But even if Sadie thought my stuff was junk—it's not, by the way, so after you bin those combats, make sure you check out my website, and I'll give you a birthday discount.'

'I'll do th—'

'But even if she did, why'd she buy it? I never asked her to. Intentionally sabotaging my business. My future. My daughter's future. To make matters worse, I'm saving up to get Jess driving lessons from Santy, you know? It's about time she learned. Twenty-one years of age. If she wants to be a makeup artist, she'll need wheels to get her from A to B. Going to weddings and photoshoots. But how is Santy going to afford to buy her lessons? Reviews like my cousin left aren't going to help bring me new customers, let me tell you.'

'I suppose not.'

'I don't know why Sadie's family think they're better than everyone else. You're an auld one, like me, Connie, so you know—'

'Steady on, Breege,' Mary Elizabeth interrupted, arriving from the garden, 'she's forty, not ninety.'

'God, I'm sorry, Connie, I didn't mean to offend you. You look younger than me, that's for sure. My makeup is everywhere, is it?'

It was, and Connie soon set about remedying the panda-like mascara smudges.

'Thanks, hun,' Breege continued, 'and, by the way, you look like a spring chicken in that outfit. I'd give you thirty, maybe, but definitely not forty! If you ever fancy making some "adult entertainment" videos, let me know!'

'Never say never, I suppose!'

'Mary Elizabeth, top me up, will you?'

'Me too,' Connie instructed her best friend, looking around the kitchen. The walls were barely visible thanks to the mountains of presents, drinks and food arriving all afternoon. Generous neighbours and well-wishers had brought some, but most were from businesses and companies, eager to shower gifts on Ireland's brightest rugby star. Delivery vans, a constant presence all day, battled for space on their narrow lane.

'I'll tell you this for nothing, Breege,' Mary Elizabeth declared, filling their glasses. 'In this world, we've to accept that there are feckers at every turn. Feckers like Liam's father, for instance.'

'Shush! Liam will hear you!'

'And now,' Mary Elizabeth continued, ignoring Connie, 'feckers like your cousin, Breege. What did you say her name was again?'

'Sadie.'

'Shady Sadie. What more proof do you need?'

'Shady Sadie! It all makes sense now.'

'I'm going to head out to Dad,' Connie interrupted. 'You met his new carer earlier, didn't you? He seems lovely.'

'And handsome,' Mary Elizabeth enthused. 'Those muscly arms! I was about to tell One-Syllable Rory to hightail it, but then remembered he has to stay because of Bosco.'

'Bosco?' Breege interrupted, 'Like the puppet?'

'What's Bosco got to do with Rory?' Connie quizzed, suspecting her best friend was up to her old tricks.

'Nothing, Curious Connie! Anyway, I'd say your dad is having a smashing time. I had a great chat with him earlier about JFK, of all people, and he seemed to be as happy as a clam at high tide.'

'Good. I'm worried about Heather, though. She doesn't deserve to be struggling with her health after everything she's done for all those foster children over the years.'

'If only Shady Sadie was more like you,' Breege said to Connie, draping an arm around her shoulder. 'So caring and considerate.'

'Can I get an "amen"?' Mary Elizabeth replied.

'Ladies, you'll have to excuse me because I'm blushing.'

She moved towards the open door and scanned the garden. The lawn resembled a war zone, with bodies sprawled everywhere, basking in the afternoon sunshine. She spotted Andy tuning his guitar to prepare for the medley of Fenian songs he invariably played during social gatherings. Connie imagined a few rousing renditions of 'Come Out, Ye Black and Tans' would make her plans to brew coffee unnecessary.

The day is young, she thought, taking a sip of her wine.

CHAPTER THIRTEEN

NOW

NEAR THE BUS stop on the outskirts of the village, Connie squats behind a fence covered in bushes and brambles. She runs the temples of her sunglasses through the mud to distract her from Kavanagh's barn, taunting her in the distance. The field, the afterparty, the violence, the vixen. The crash.

Connie had received her driving licence in her late twenties, thanks to her father's insistence.

'You won't know yourself! The independence!' he'd claimed.

Connie joked that he was concerned about his own independence. In truth, he was getting older and wanted his daughter to be self-sufficient. But even before that fateful night, her relationship with driving had been problematic. When her dependency on prescription medication was at its worst, she often drove under the influence. There had been a near-miss with a lollipop lady in Bettystown, which could have proven fatal if the woman hadn't been a member of the local karate club, equipping her with impressive reflexes.

The situation had become so precarious that Liam, still a teenager, took the car keys from her until she proved to have total control of her faculties. Her success in 'overcoming' her addiction was the principal reason Liam had used the contract money from the national team to reward her with a car on her birthday. The shiny black Mini Cooper came straight off the conveyor belt with a joke registration plate that read 'MAMMY MAGUIRE'.

One, two, three. She counts the number of blackbirds flying above her. *Four, five, six.*

'Mam,' Liam says, appearing beside her. 'It's not a good idea to wait here. Not only does the entire village know you're back, but so does the country after someone shared videos online. I'd say those reporters have uploaded all those images they took of you in the graveyard to their websites by now.'

'Already?'

'It only takes seconds, so you need to get out of here. Everyone knows you can't drive anymore. Breege doesn't have to be Sherlock Holmes to work out that you're hiding beside a bus stop.'

'Where else can I wait? I can't go into the wood because the bus will pass if I don't stop it in time. And even if I move to another stop further away from the village, she'll eventually find me.'

'And that's exactly what has just happened, Mam.'

A car screeches, a door slams shut, and high-heeled boots march across the road. Connie closes her eyes and accepts what is about to transpire.

'Look at me! Look at me!'

But Connie doesn't need to open her eyes to see this woman's face. The glimpse she caught of Breege in the courthouse will be ingrained in her mind for life: the grief, the anguish, the torment.

'You're even more heartless than we thought, coming back to the village as if nothing had happened.'

Connie keeps her focus on the ground but nods in agreement.

'Don't I wish I was locked up in prison like you, hidden away from everything,' Breege continues. 'But I was here, having to pick up the pieces.'

'I know, I know.'

'You know what? You'll *never* know what it's like choosing a coffin from a catalogue for your baby girl. Will she prefer white, brown or dark brown? Spending hours deciding on an outfit for her—the stress of not knowing whether she'd have approved.'

Connie keeps her arms by her side; she won't attempt to defend herself from the inevitable punches.

'Mam!' Liam shouts. 'What are you doing? You need to run, or she'll kill you!'

But, for some reason, Breege has yet to throw a single slap. Connie doesn't know why, seeing as violence is second nature to her.

'You'll never know what it's like getting the undertakers to use makeup that was no better than that mud on the ground so that all her cuts and bruises could be hidden,' Breege continues. 'You'll never know what it's like having to choose readings and hymns for mass. Having to argue with the priest when he says we can't play her favourite pop song in the church because they're now against the rules.'

Now, Connie thinks, *now she'll hit me, kick me, punch me.* But Breege maintains her distance.

'You'll never know what it's like having to keep her bedroom door locked to avoid seeing all her things. All the dolls and teddies she'd saved from when she was a child. Jesus Christ, she was still a child when you murdered her. Why, why, why did you get behind the wheel? Why couldn't you have stayed in bed?'

'Hit me!' Connie screams at Breege, finally standing up, her arms outstretched. 'Hit me!'

Liam stands between the two women. 'Mam, what are you doing?'

'You'd like a few slaps, so you don't have to listen— *actually listen*—to what I've to say. To understand what we went through. Because that's what you do, isn't it, Connie Maguire? You always find some way to escape the shite in your life. Popping pills, drinking, eating, making stupid jokes and now, getting a good hiding. But I won't give you that satisfaction.'

'Please, that's enough, Breege. Please.'

'You'll never know what it's like to sit by her grave, begging her to forgive me for not protecting her. Not keeping her alive. Not being a better mam to her. God knows I wanted to be, but I had my demons. Unlike you, I was addressing them. I was trying to change—my new online shop, remember? I just wanted to be a better mother to her. That's all I ever wanted. To be a better mother.'

Connie furiously grabs Breege's hand. 'Hit me! Please, hit me!'

'Mam, run away!' Liam pleads.

Horns sound from passing cars, adding to the frenzy.

'Punch me,' Connie begs, 'kick me, pull my hair! Anything—*just hit me*!'

Finally, Breege complies. A full-force slap, right across her face. Punches, lots of them. Kicks to her stomach, lots of them. While doubled over, gasping for air, Connie hears muffled voices. Words like 'murderer', 'junkie' and 'twenty-one' jump out. Then, silence: Breege is gone.

'Are you okay?'

Connie doesn't recognise the warm, kind voice. She momentarily thinks it belongs to Teddy. But when her ears stop ringing, she realises that the accent isn't local. African, maybe. The man from the bus that morning, whose face she recognised from somewhere.

'It's okay, she's gone.'

The pain, which Connie had momentarily found relieving, is now overbearing. She can't work out where it hurts the most: her face, her ribs, her lower back.

'Let me give you a hand. It's not safe here. That crazy woman—'

'She's not crazy. I need to get a bus to Dublin.'

'We need to get you to a hospital.'

'No, no! I'm fine,' Connie pathetically lies, trying to curb the bleeding from above her right eye. 'I have to get the bus. If I miss this one, I'll have to wait another two hours.'

'Do you think any driver will let you on in your condition? At least let me bring you to the site. We've got a first aid kit there. Some painkillers. Although, you need to—'

'A first aid kit will be enough. But no painkillers.'

* * *

Connie sits in a small, musty cabin positioned in the centre of a construction site. She isn't sure of its exact location, but it's within walking—or limping—distance of the bus stop. Since the Celtic Tiger, there has been unending development across Dublin's commuter belt. Furious locals could barely keep up with the village's ever-changing appearance.

Abeo introduces himself and spends the next twenty minutes cleaning and bandaging Connie's many wounds. Despite her form, Connie knows what sits in front of her: a first aid kit bulging with pills and tablets. She's unsure of the medication's purpose—perhaps headaches, upset stomachs or hay fever. But no matter their appeal or effectiveness, she won't touch them, even though every doctor would prescribe her something to numb the unbearable pain.

'I'd offer you a biscuit,' he says, handing her some tea, 'but you probably don't have an appetite.'

She smiles, touched by his kindness. 'I'm not sure if I'll be able to drink either.' The simple act of lifting a cup is a challenge.

'I've seen many assaults over the years, but that was one of the worst.'

'Those people probably weren't grieving parents.'

'Are you sure you don't want me to call the police?'

'Of course not. She deserved to do that.'

'No one deserves to do that.'

'Well, she did.'

'If you say so. At least let me take you to A&E. There could be internal bleeding. Or other injuries.'

'I'll be fine.'

'Where are you staying? Can I call someone? Not the police, but someone who can take care of you.'

'Just give me a minute to steady myself, and I'll be gone.'

As much as she dreads spending another second in the guesthouse with reporters circling outside, Connie doesn't want to return to Dublin too late. The capital is unfamiliar to her. Since childhood, she's tried to avoid crowds. While devoted to her son's career, attending Liam's early rugby games amongst the throngs of supporters was always a challenge. The anxiety medication helped, and when she needed a boost, Connie took a little extra.

'Where is she?'

Round two.

Abeo rushes to the window. 'There are about four of them in a white van. They're behind the security gate.'

The cabin door bursts open, and Simon, the construction manager, storms in.

'What the hell are you doing here? I can't have any trouble—I've already had those health and safety pricks sniffing around.'

Connie steels herself for what lies ahead. 'I'll go.'

'Where?' Simon cuts in, assisting her to her feet while watching the growing threat outside.

'The bus to Dublin.'

'Have you a death wish? There's a crowd of madmen out there.'

A rock crashes through the window as if to endorse his claims.

Connie peeps over Simon's shoulder and sees builders arguing with an army of vigilantes standing behind a tall gate. She recognises them, people she once called neighbours and friends. All those occasions they had spent together: birthday parties, weddings, anniversaries. Some had even been guests at her party, invited by Breege and Andy. For better or worse, they'd been a community.

Simon grabs keys from a hook. 'You need to follow me.'

Abeo takes Connie by the arm; she winces before giving her standard 'I'm fine' response. They struggle to maintain Simon's speed as he races across the muddy site, jumping over puddles.

'Don't go to Dublin,' he advises, rounding a generator and stack of pallets. 'Go off-grid. Until it all calms down.'

'Where will I go?' She, along with many people working directly and indirectly for the prison service, had asked this question repeatedly over the past few months. But Connie couldn't visualise a future for herself. Not in the village, not in Dublin, not with Liam. Not anywhere.

'Go to my uncle's old caravan park.' Simon suggests, leading them into a makeshift car park in an adjacent field. 'If you put your foot down, it's about a four-hour journey. Abeo, you've been there.'

Connie notices the shock of this suggestion across her new friend's face.

'Thanks,' she says to Simon, 'but I can't drive anymore.'

'Abeo will take you.'

She vaguely remembers Teddy telling her about an invitation he'd received on the morning of her birthday.

'I'm not sure the caravan park would be suitable for a woman—alone,' Abeo replies. 'The time we went, there was broken glass, no showers, no electricity.'

The roars from the mob grow louder; the builders and gates can only hold them back for so long.

'Get as far away from here as possible,' Simon continues, opening the car door and forcing Connie in.

'Why are you helping me, Simon?'

'God, does it matter?'

'It does to me.'

'Eli, my son. You were very good to him at school.'

'He gave me flowers. For my birthday.'

'I should really be annoyed with you because I'm sick of hearing that stupid falling asleep joke.' Simon takes a breath. 'He doesn't touch anyone or allow anyone to touch him. But he always had a hug for you. The little lad hasn't been the same since you left. Let us help you for a change. Now go!'

Two men, Jess' cousins, finally breach the gate and storm into the construction site. Behind them, the photographers from the graveyard, never ones to miss a front-page opportunity, click their cameras. Abeo reverses over the muddy field towards the exit. Once out onto the main road, he turns to Connie. 'Are you sure about this?'

Breege's words dominate her mind. 'Yes, absolutely.'

Abeo puts his foot down on the accelerator and drives west.

CHAPTER FOURTEEN
SATURDAY, LATE AFTERNOON

CONNIE HAD JUST said goodbye to her father and his carer when the professional photographer and journalist arrived at the party. The girlfriend of one of Liam's teammates, a supposed marketing queen, had failed to mention that the many expensive flourishes scattered across the garden—the photo booth, piñata, floral birdcages and decorative flamingos—were courtesy of a glossy magazine. In exchange, they required a selection of images and exclusive interviews.

By now, everyone was in high spirits, especially the birthday girl, as they welcomed the unexpected arrivals with their cameras and ring lights. The guests gathered behind Liam and Jess, cheering them on as they pretended to smash the piñata dangling from the tree. Connie was impressed by their ease in taking orders from the demanding photographer.

'They're absolute naturals,' Mary Elizabeth said, giving Connie's hair a boost. 'The Irish Posh and Becks. Cover models, the pair of them.'

'Do you know why they look so good together?' Connie added. 'Because they *are* so good together.'

'Cupid brought his A-game when he introduced those two lovebirds, that's for sure.'

The journalist beckoned Connie into the living room for a chat—'a few, easy-breezy questions, nothing to worry about.'

Four hours earlier, Connie would have run to the hills at the prospect of doing an interview, especially one set to feature in a glossy magazine. Now, she embraced the attention, linking arms with the publicist as they strolled through the kitchen and into the living room.

'I haven't much experience answering questions like yours,' Connie began once they'd settled on the sofa. 'But I'll do my best to be as interesting as possible!'

'Don't worry, it won't be too serious,' the journalist assured her, readily accepting a glass of cava. 'I plan to call the article "The Wonderful Life of Connie Maguire". I hope you know how many women across Ireland envy you.'

'Me?'

'Yes, you.'

'The Wonderful Life of Connie Maguire', Connie repeated to herself, goosebumps hijacking her arms.

'I don't read many celebrity interviews, but I know how exciting their lives can be. Red carpets and award shows every other night. I feel I deserve a prize if I remember to use conditioner after shampoo! So, let me know if my answers need to be more jazzy!'

The journalist switched on the voice recorder. 'Are you okay with this interview being recorded?' Connie nodded. 'First off, how does the mother of a world-class athlete keep in shape?'

'I'm yoga mad!' Connie immediately replied, delighted to be viewed as fit and healthy.

'I can tell. You have a lovely glow.'

'Do I?' Connie couldn't believe that a journalist who'd interviewed the A-to-Z of Irish celebrities had described her as glowing. 'Thank you,' she replied, remembering her mantra: new beginnings. Maybe those days of diminishing herself were truly in the past.

'Yoga is worlds apart from rugby, isn't it?' the journalist continued.

'You should have seen me when I started—tumbling and falling with bruises all over my poor body. You'd have thought I'd been in a scrum with Liam!'

'Speaking of Liam, what do you think the secret to his success is?'

Connie studied the many trophies, plaques and medals dotted around the room: years of Liam's victories. The party and interview were lovely ways to celebrate all her son had accomplished in his career.

'Many people have asked me this question, and I never know what to say. You'd probably have to ask him or his managers. But I know that I'm incredibly proud, and whatever happens now that he's joining the Ireland squad, I want him to be happy. Both on and off the pitch. He has worked so hard over the years.'

'In what way?'

'Up at the crack of dawn every morning to go for a run or hit the gym. His diet, his focus, his passion. His commitment, discipline, motivation, sense of camaraderie. I'm gushing now.'

'And what mother wouldn't be? Where do you think he got those traits? From you, I'd imagine.'

Connie was determined not to let herself down by criticising herself. 'Who knows,' she said, 'again, all I'll say is that being his mother fills me with pride every single day. And I will continue to support him in whatever way I can.'

'When I spoke to Liam a few minutes ago, I asked him the same question about where he got it from—his gift. I'll read back what he said, will I? Although, be warned, you might need a few tissues handy.'

The journalist flicked through her notes before finding Liam's quote. '"I owe all my success to my mam, who raised me as a single mother and dedicated her life to me. Anything I am is because of her. She'll always be with me, and I'll give my everything for her. People kindly say that my sporting talent is my greatest gift, but to be honest, my mother is my greatest gift. And I'll forever treasure her."'

As Connie allowed her son's beautiful words to wash over her, she heard a sudden bang in the garden, followed by a commotion. Excusing herself, she spotted Liam storming across the lawn, upturning a flamingo and disappearing along the side of the cottage.

'Is everything all right?' Connie asked Mary Elizabeth and Jess when she emerged outside and noticed the piñata now lying scattered across the lawn.

'Don't get upset,' Mary Elizabeth began. 'Liam realised Nick was nowhere to be seen, so he called him.'

'Nick wasn't particularly friendly and had no interest in returning,' Jess added. 'To make matters worse, I think Liam was about to propose to me.'

'What?' Connie and Mary Elizabeth replied in unison.

'I think so. A box fell out of his pocket when he was tying his shoes earlier. Heather picked it up and gave it back to him. I pretended not to see. Then, during the photo shoot, he said he had something to ask me but wanted his dad to be here first.'

'I'll have to go after him.'

'No, Connie, I'll go,' Jess said, heading off. 'I'm sure he just needs to count to ten.'

'That absolute bastard,' Connie fumed to Mary Elizabeth. 'It's awful to say, but if someone punched Nick's "oh-so-handsome face", I'd—'

'Shake their hand?'

'And give them one of Liam's trophies.'

The journalist emerged from the house. 'We'll let you know when the interview will run.'

Connie smiled politely, desperate to keep up appearances.

'The Wonderful Life of Connie Maguire'—if only they knew the truth.

CHAPTER FIFTEEN
NOW

CONNIE AND ABEO sit in silence, surrounded by smells familiar to builders' vehicles: paint, white spirit and wood chippings. The sun-bleached air freshener, hanging from the rear-view mirror, shrugs in defeat, conceding there's little use competing with the dominant fragrances in the car. They have managed to create a safe distance between themselves and their pursuers thanks to a lorry casually making deliveries to a gardening centre, but they aren't taking anything for granted, especially Connie.

Holding her handbag tightly, she attempts to distract herself by focusing on the countryside. Meath is famous for its land, and this afternoon, it looks incredibly lush after the rain. As the car whizzes past house after house, she envies the owners tending to their gardens or returning from shopping, knowing she'll never experience a normal life again. Connie can vividly recall every item she purchased when last in a supermarket, two nights before her birthday. Panicked that the house wasn't party-ready, the perfectionist had forced Mary Elizabeth to accompany her to Drogheda for a last-minute shopping splurge—'splurge' being the operative word. The overwhelmed cashier even commented on the mountain of cleaning products piled high on the conveyor belt.

'I hope you haven't murdered somebody!' he joked.

Little did Connie realise she'd soon be on the front page of every newspaper in the country. People obsess about female killers, and her crimes were, of course, even more appealing to ruthless editors and insatiable readers because of her connection to a rising sports star and the deceased, not to mention the reels of footage from the party showing her intoxicated state.

Connie feels blood seeping through the bandage covering her eye. Now the initial adrenaline is wearing off, her many injuries ransack her body. The attack was cyclonic, but she remembers every kick, every punch, every slap. Breege had earned it all. Her words, too, echo in Connie's mind.

'You'll never know what it's like to sit by her grave, begging her to forgive me for not protecting her. Not keeping her alive.'

'Are we going on a road trip?'

Connie looks at her son, perched on a tin of paint in the back, his face dominated by a broad smile.

'I should have brought my swimming togs, what with all this sunshine,' he adds, peering out the window. 'Four seasons in one day.'

'I thought you didn't like getting wet! The struggles I had getting you into a bath!'

'Sometimes, you forget I've grown up since then.'

'But you'll always be my little boy, and I won't apologise for saying so.'

'The only person who should be apologising today is Breege after the number she did on you. And don't justify it as you did to your new friend—she certainly does not deserve to beat anyone up, least of all my mother.'

'Do you recognise that place?' Connie says, pointing at a signpost on their right-hand side.

'Isn't that Kenny's bog? Are we in Westmeath already? Your man certainly knows how to put the foot down, fair play to him.'

'He's my guardian angel.'

'Remember when Kenny had those Christmas angels on the roof of his house, and two fell during a thunderstorm and knocked Granddad out cold!'

'You were only about four. There's nothing wrong with your memory.'

'Actually, that isn't to my advantage these days,' he replies. 'I remember too much. Training hasn't been going great. I find it hard to concentrate, remembering everything that happened that night. And, of course, everything that happened afterwards. I don't think I've slept properly in twenty-one months. The other lads aren't too impressed with my performance. They understand the horrible situation, but something will have to change.'

'As if they'd ever drop you—aren't you the country's golden boy? One of the youngest ever to be capped for Ireland? Even at your worst, you're still one of the best in the world.'

'If only everyone thought as highly of me as you do.'

'I'll always be your biggest fan if that counts for anything.'

'It counts for everything.' He gently places a hand on her shoulder. 'I miss you, Mam.'

'Not nearly as much as I miss you, my love.'

Connie feels a hand on her shoulder—this time, a real one.

'Are you all right?' Abeo asks. 'Your mouth's moving, but you're not saying anything. You might have a concussion. Let's go to a hospital.'

Connie offers him a warm smile. 'I'm fine, thanks to you.'

Abeo appears unconvinced. 'If you need me to stop at any stage for something to eat or even fresh air, please tell me.' He turns the radio on, but dried paint scattered across it makes the buttons difficult to operate. Eventually, he settles on some classical music.

'It's far from Beethoven you were reared, Mam,' Liam teases from behind. 'Why don't you ask him to put on a bit of Philomena Begley or Nathan Carter—they're more your style!'

Connie doesn't get a chance to scold her teasing son: the chilling sound of a van horn heralds the return of her old friends.

They've caught up.

Connie surveys the car and its arsenal of makeshift weapons—hammers, screwdrivers, nail guns and blades. She dreads the prospect of having to use them.

'Connie, where's the nearest police station?'

'Kilbeggan, I'd say. About another ten or fifteen minutes.'

After checking her side mirror, Connie realises there is just a single motorcycle between them. She makes out three faces in the van but imagines others are lurking behind them. Abeo can't maintain pole position for another ten minutes; the large van could easily force them off the road.

'Too far,' Abeo says. 'Any other ideas?'

'Let me out.'

'What?' he replies, his accent thickening under pressure.

'It's me they want. I'm putting you in danger.'

'I'm not letting you out.'

'Abeo, they will hurt us. You don't know what these people are like. "These people"—listen to me. These people are my people. Or used to be. If only you knew what happened.'

'I do know, Connie.'

'Of course, the papers, radio, television.'

The van overtakes the motorcyclist and is quickly gaining ground.

'Not just that,' Abeo says. 'I've not been truthful with you.'

Connie stiffens. When he'd last visited her in prison, Liam warned about the lengths unscrupulous reporters were prepared to go to get an exclusive.

'Don't trust anyone,' he'd advised.

'You won't remember me,' Abeo continues. 'I was your father's carer. I was at your party to drop him off and pick him up.'

'I knew I recognised you on the bus. Yes, you were there that day. And so kind. I remember. We all thought that about you. Kind.'

'You were all wrong. I was stealing money from your dad.'

'What?'

'A nurse caught me. I was having problems with my family. It doesn't matter because there are no excuses.'

Connie struggles to reconcile this protective man beside her with a petty thief. 'I'm sure you had no choice.'

'Your father had a choice. He asked everyone to forget it ever happened. It was probably the clearest I'd ever seen him.'

'He was always a man for second chances.'

'That's why I want to help you. You deserve a second chance.'

'Stealing money hardly justifies putting your life at risk.'

'That's my choice to make.'

As he utters those words, the van slaps the car's bumper, thrusting them forward.

'The bog!' Liam suggests, reappearing behind them.

'The bog!' Connie echoes. 'It's up ahead. A friend owns it.'

'What are you thinking?'

'There's a height restriction barrier,' she replies, measuring up the van, now almost at their side. 'They won't pass under it.'

'It's not a truck.'

'The barrier is low. Kenny installed it to prevent thefts. People were helping themselves—' She stops herself short.

'You don't think the van will make it through?'

'Definitely not, Mam,' Liam insists.

'Definitely not.'

'But could they go around it?'

'No, there are walls and trees.'

'It's not like we've got many choices,' Abeo decides after receiving another bang from the van. 'Tell me when to—'

'Turn!' Liam roars.

'Turn!'

Abeo steers the wheel to the left, propelling the car through a narrow ditch and landing on a waterlogged field. The van behind them doesn't anticipate such a sudden move; stunned, it continues along the main road. Abeo drives the car across the soggy terrain before merging onto a long, dusty track.

'Are you okay?'

'Fine. Just keep going.'

Connie hoped the surprise re-routing into the field would create a distance between the two vehicles, but stealing a glance at the rear-view mirror, she spots the van bursting through the ditch. The excitement from their spontaneous diversion makes way for a measure of reality. There was protection on the main road, a public space with other cars zooming up and down. Here, they are isolated and vulnerable. They close in on the barrier in front of them.

It is low, very low, she evaluates, confident the van won't be able to clear it. The barrier is bookended by long walls that divide the fields and bogs; only the occasional tree breaks the monotony of the grey stone.

'We're almost there. You're doing great.' Connie is sure these token words of encouragement only serve to distract Abeo. Still, she needs an opportunity to say something to release the pain coursing through her body, exacerbated by the uneven terrain. This terrifying chase will be over if they can manage another fifteen seconds.

'You've got to be kidding!'

Connie doesn't need to ask the cause of Abeo's alarm because she can hear it for herself: the car's overworked engine.

'Don't cut out on us now,' he pleads.

He keeps his gaze straight ahead, but a shadow falls on them from their left. Not only has the van caught up, but it has momentum on its side. All it has to do is swerve in front of them, and it's game over.

'The only way to stop them blocking us is …' Abeo says. 'Hold tight!'

Jockeying for first position, he pulls the wheel to his left. The car collides with the front of the van, and even though the car now spirals, Abeo has the advantage of knowing this would happen and steadies himself. This sudden impact takes their pursuers unawares, and before they can react, the van crashes into the wall.

Following a glance at Connie to ensure she isn't hurt— 'I'm fine, keep going!'—Abeo holds the wheel straight and careens towards the barrier. Not even the sound of the roof scraping against the metal barrier undermines their relief as they coast towards safety.

CHAPTER SIXTEEN
THEN, SATURDAY EVENING

GERRY WAS BUSY in the kitchen preparing another batch of sangria, his husband's recipe. Beside him, a distracted Connie stared at her phone, awaiting an update. Her state of zen had evaporated after Liam's abrupt exit. Gerry handed her a glass.

'Here you go, darling—you look like you need it.'

After accepting the drink, Connie's phone finally pinged. Jess explained that she and Liam had enjoyed a head-clearing ramble along the old canal and were now on their way back. She'd blamed their delay on bumping into Mandy Waldron and her new dog. Jess was great at diffusing sticky situations; her experience with Breege stood to her when dealing with a crisis. If she hadn't pursued a career in beauty, the young woman would have made a great politician.

Standing by the door, Connie allowed the sunshine to warm her face. With Liam returning, the day's celebrations were finally back on track. Even Breege was on her best behaviour, playing a game of Giant Jenga with her cousins in the garden while Andy impressed Liam's friends with a muted version of 'The Foggy Dew'.

Connie wasn't a gambling woman, but she would have bet her final euro that Mary Elizabeth would invite a 'someone I'd like you to meet' guest. Before finishing a mouthful of Gerry's sangria, she heard a roar from the side of the cottage: 'Connie, there's someone I'd like you to meet!'

She would need a calculator to count the number of introductions Mary Elizabeth had made over the decades. Maybe her personal Cupid had oversold her looks or personality, but most of the exchanges had ended as soon as they began. Her mother once claimed that if her daughter had any good qualities, 'losing weight or choosing men' weren't either of them. Connie never disagreed.

'You need to put yourself out there,' Mary Elizabeth would always encourage or, in later years, complain. 'You're gorgeous—any man would kill to have you. Besides, you give too much of yourself to Liam. What will happen when he heads off to become an international sports star? Empty nest syndrome, that's all I'm going to say. You might think I'm annoying now, but you'll thank me in the coming years when you've got an itch on your back and need someone to scratch it.'

Connie received more male attention after Liam's career soared, but that proved more of a hindrance than a help, as she discovered a few months after Helga died. Mary Elizabeth had dragged her to a wedding, claiming there was someone she'd like her to meet. It was a rare occasion when Connie had felt free from self-loathing without the help of medication. Her mother's death certainly played a part in liberating her from her inhibitions. However, this sudden joy was temporary. When her 'date' slinked behind her during 'Rock the Boat', she thought the dance would end with a kiss. Instead, it ended with a request for tickets to an upcoming rugby match and an introduction to Liam—'the talk of the Irish sporting scene', as he'd described the then-teenager.

Maybe tonight will be different. New beginnings.

Bosco, similar in age to Connie, wore thick, black-rimmed glasses and a bushy beard. While greeting each other, she noticed his green shirt still bore the price tag.

At least he's made an effort.

There were no signs of nerves as he kissed her cheek, just a pleasant fragrance that reminded Connie of the old leather chairs in Kenny's home. If first impressions counted for anything, this latest blind date scored highly. Mary Elizabeth introduced the pair before disappearing into the kitchen with a mischievous glint in her eye.

Bosco handed Connie a present. 'Happy birthday.'

'What is it?' she asked, trying to understand why the words 'Connie Major' were emblazoned across a certificate.

'I'm an astronomy nerd, so I named a star after you to mark the occasion,' he explained.

On a day replete with thoughtful presents, Connie wished there were more effective ways of expressing her gratitude.

'You shouldn't have gone to so much trouble.'

'There wasn't much to it other than registering your name on a website. But if it wins me brownie points, we can say I travelled up into the galaxy with my pen to handwrite "Connie Major" on the star.'

'In that case, I hope your jet lag isn't too bad.'

Nightfall wasn't due for another two hours, but Connie became giddy at the thought of searching the sky for the star.

My star.

'Get the poor guy a drink!' Mary Elizabeth shouted from the kitchen.

'Of course,' Connie said to Bosco, 'and some food? After your gorgeous present, you deserve—'

'The *star* treatment?'

'Words right out of my mouth!'

CHAPTER SEVENTEEN

NOW

'TURN RIGHT AFTER that large sycamore.'

Kenny's property is an elegant Edwardian red-brick, with a balcony, porch and side-hinged casement windows. Green ivy partially covers the walls, and although it's late June, smoke escapes from a chimney, the perks of owning a bog. As a young, ambitious entrepreneur, Kenny co-owned a whiskey distillery in County Westmeath, which had proven popular in Asia. After selling his shares two decades later, exhausted from fourteen-hour flights, he and Heather exchanged life in the fast lane for a quieter pace in the midlands countryside.

Connie and Abeo examine the car.

'I'll give you the money to repair it,' she assures Abeo. 'Dad's car must have been lower.'

'It was!'

Connie and Abeo look towards the balcony on the second floor, where Kenny stands, smiling and sporting a neck brace.

'Kenny! I hope you don't mind us stopping by.'

'Of course not. I've been waiting for you to call every hour since you were released. Anyway, Heather is having a nap before her physio, but let me get my glasses, and I'll come down and put the kettle on. You'll need to give me about a week.' He points at the white brace, which perfectly complements his beard. 'This will teach me to tie my shoelaces properly!'

As Kenny disappears, Connie turns to Abeo. 'Could you hide the car inside there?' She points towards a line of outhouses. 'I'd hate if I brought any danger here.'

'No need to explain. I'll check the engine and knock on the door when I'm finished. Be prepared—the car mightn't be able to take us to the caravan park.'

Alone, Connie studies the familiar garden, notably the willow tree, with its long limbs swaying in the breeze, commanding everyone's attention. In front of it lies a flowerbed of vibrant roses, her favourite. She walks to the bench where she often sat to read, relaxing after a morning helping on the bog. She always felt at home here and often wondered whether the many invites to stay were her father's way of offering Connie a reprieve from her mother. On many other occasions, Kenny and Heather attempted to convince Helga to be kinder to everyone, but their words didn't yield success, apart from reinforcing Connie's love for them, her surrogate parents.

She remembers her last journey here. One night, her father suddenly woke, realising that he'd never returned a rope to Kenny. He phoned Connie, full of panic, and insisted he return it immediately.

'We can go down together tomorrow, Dad—it's almost five in the morning! We can even bring Liam and make a day of it.'

But her father, who'd recently become impatient, wanted to complete the task without delay.

'It's about respect, Connie,' he argued. 'You should always return what's not yours.'

Alarmed by his forceful demands, Connie eventually relented and crept out of the house without waking Liam, not due in the gym for another hour. It was a good job she'd accompanied her father, given his erratic driving. When Kenny insisted that the rope didn't belong to him, she accepted it was the beginning of the end for her father.

'My slide is gone!' Liam exclaims, now appearing beside his mother. 'Or did I do something to it?'

'If I recall correctly, you knocked it over with a rugby ball, and it smashed into the shed. Kenny and Dad didn't give out to you because they realised how talented you were.'

'Enough about me, that guy seems nice,' Liam teases, pointing towards Abeo. 'It's time you got yourself a fella!'

'You sound like Mary Elizabeth.'

'That devoted father of mine abandoned you how many years ago? I'm twenty-five now, so that would make it twenty-six. Look, I'm not trying to pimp my mother out, but you're entitled to romance. And who better than your chauffeur with the thick, curly hair? And "gorgeous muscles", as Mary Elizabeth described them at the barbecue.'

Connie's last date was on the night of her birthday: Bosco, an astronomy fanatic with a witty sense of humour. The night might have turned out differently if she'd remained with him and allowed him to impress her with his knowledge of Polaris, Sirius and Connie Major.

Liam takes hold of her trembling hands. 'Mam, you're shaking.'

'It'll pass.'

He places a hand on her face. 'I hope you know—'

'I'll tell you what I know: I should never have come back. The hurt I caused to Breege and her family all over again. What was I thinking?'

'That's a good question, Mam. What were you thinking?'

Connie knows she could have avoided all this unpleasantness if she'd had the sense to remain in Dublin and allow the photo to fade into memory. Whenever Liam played poorly over the years, the supportive mother would remind him: 'What's done is done. Forget the past, and now, look ahead.' If only she could have taken this advice on board.

'I just needed my photo,' she continues, seeing it in her bag. 'It reassures me. Some connection with you before everything fell apart. Once I got the idea into my head this morning, I couldn't shake it. Just like the day of my birthday when I convinced myself that I …'

'Needed those tablets.'

The front door creaks open.

'Sorry for keeping you, Concepta; I couldn't even compete with a terrapin these days. Dear God, your face!'

With the benefit of glasses, Kenny sees the damage done to his best friend's only child. 'Are you all right? What on earth happened to you? Do you need me to call a doctor?'

'It looks much worse than it is,' Connie lies.

'What happened to you?'

'You probably won't believe me if I say that I also tripped on my shoelaces. Anyway, I'm fine, don't worry. A cuppa would be lovely, though.'

'Consider it done,' he replies, failing to hide his concern.

Following him inside, Connie is comforted by his avuncular voice and the familiarity of his home. She inhales the distinctive smell of old leather.

Everything's the same.

Of course, everything isn't the same, and nothing ever would be again. Connie hobbles past the coat rack, barely visible thanks to all the outerwear hanging from it, and follows the smell of bacon into the kitchen. Kenny and Heather treated themselves to a fry-up every Friday afternoon or Fryday, as they'd christened it. Given how little Heather ate at the birthday party, Connie imagines Kenny now enjoys the lion's share.

'Is your friend not coming in?' Kenny asks, offering Connie a seat. 'There's plenty in the house to eat if you're hungry. I'll throw down a few sausages.'

'We're fine, Kenny, I promise.' Her mind races back to the breakfast Andy threw at her earlier that day in the café; it seems like a lifetime ago.

'If you say so, Concepta. Just a cup of tea, then?'

'That sounds perfect. Maybe make a pot in case Abeo—'

'Is that his name?'

'Yes, and one of the nicest men I've ever met.'

'Present company excluded, of course. Your dad had a carer called Abeo.'

Connie hadn't expected Kenny to know that information, but it makes sense: they were best friends until the end.

'Although,' Kenny continues, placing three mugs on the wooden table and clearing newspapers out of the way, 'I don't think I'd have described that particular Abeo as one of the nicest men I'd ever met. He robbed your dad, the nurse told me. Quite a lot of money, I'll hasten to add. Straight after the …'

'Crash?'

'Yes. Your father claimed he'd returned the money to him, but sure, he'd no idea what was happening. He didn't even know what day of the week it was.'

Connie glances out the window. Thankfully, Abeo is hidden behind the open bonnet.

'Speaking of money, do you have enough, Concepta?'

'Yes, Liam has seen to that.'

'No surprise there. Well, here's a couple of bob.'

'No, honestly, Kenny, I don't need anything.'

'For petrol.' He places ten fifty euro notes into her hand. 'And an ice cream—make the best of the fine day. Besides, I won a few bob on the gee-gees but say nothing to herself!'

'Tell me, how is she? Her new hip—has it been a success?'

Kenny uses the distraction of the kettle coming to its boil to choose his words correctly.

'She's slowing down. Not that she'd dream of admitting as much. You know what my darling wife is like—as stubborn as that bull in McCafferty's field. She's still battling day after day. But her lungs are worn out.'

As he places the teapot and jug of milk on the table, Connie notes that Kenny, too, has slowed down. His hearing, however, has improved, thanks to the hearing aids tucked discreetly in his ear.

'Your neck? It wasn't because you forgot to tie your shoelaces, was it?'

Kenny would shake his head if he had the physical ability. Instead, his pained expression reveals all that Connie needs to know.

'She fell down the stairs. I was in front of her. But you know what? If I hadn't, Heather mightn't have come away with just a couple of scratches. She mightn't have come away from it at all.'

As she struggles to pour the tea, Connie hears faint steps cross the hallway. It's Prince, Heather's treasured ginger Persian cat. Unlike Connie, he has put on weight since they last saw each other. As a tip of the hat to his lofty name, he ignores the guest and makes a beeline for his food bowl, where leftover bacon awaits him.

'At least this little scamp hasn't lost any of his giddy-up, that's for sure,' Kenny jokes, petting the cat, an unappreciated gesture if Prince's high-pitched, go-away meows are anything to go by.

'You could always get some help,' Connie suggests, although she knows Kenny and Heather are as bad as each other when asking for anything.

'So they can rob us the way that lad robbed your poor dad?'

Connie looks outside. The car bonnet continues to conceal Abeo, but for how much longer? As much as she needs to be in Kenny's company today, she knows her visit must be brief. A heated exchange between the pair would be unbearable.

'We'll muddle on,' Kenny adds philosophically, offering some sugar. 'We are some sorry sight today—you, me and Heather!'

'You can say that again.'

'We certainly are some sorry sight today—you, me and Heather!'

Connie smiles. She inherited her love of corny jokes from Kenny.

'Stay a while,' Kenny continues. 'Please. I know Heather would love to have you around, and I'd like to call our doctor to look at your injuries properly.'

His voice suddenly breaks. 'Sometimes, I wake up and think it was a dream—a nightmare. I still can't ... And then I torment myself for not being there, for leaving the party early.'

'Kenny, you're the last person to blame.'

'I'm worried about you, Concepta. Say you'll stay.'

'Another time. I'd like that very much.'

'Will you be joining that superstar son of yours in the Algarve?'

'You've spoken to him?'

'Daily. He's even more worried about you than we are. I had to convince him not to return—he was about to board a flight yesterday. You'll call him, won't you?'

Before she can reply, a glass shatters upstairs, resulting in a volley of colourful expletives.

'Her body might be slowing down, but her mouth is as potty as ever,' Kenny quips, rising to his feet and taking the dustpan and brush that hangs on a press.

'Let me go up,' Connie says. 'I'd like to say a quick hello.'

'Of course, but maybe introduce yourself before entering the room. She might get startled.'

Connie glimpses Abeo out the window and knows she mustn't delay too long with Heather. With the help of the handrail, she ascends the stairs as quickly as her wretched body allows, passing several photographs of both families on the wall. Picnics on the bog, singsongs around campfires, rugby matches up and down the country. Because her current state is so tragic, she views those earlier years in such a positive light. In reality, they were also dull with pain: her mother's abuse constantly ringing in her ears, being a lonely, single parent. Why else would she have gravitated towards prescription medication?

What Breege said earlier was right—'You always find some way to escape the shite in your life.'

Connie eventually reaches the landing and notes the porcelain cats sitting in menageries. How cruel life can be. Heather and Kenny, natural parents, could never conceive together after she contracted tuberculosis in her thirties, a sad situation that Heather would often reference to justify her love for animals. The couple fostered many children over the years, which mostly proved to be a positive experience for all involved. There was one child they had hoped to adopt, who was the primary catalyst for Kenny's decision to sell his distillery and uproot to the countryside. But a distant relative appeared and took the boy off to Australia. Heather had never gotten over the disappointment.

'Heather,' Connie says at the doorway. 'It's me.'

'Connie? Connie, dear heart, come here to me.'

The softness of her voice soothes Connie instantly. They hold each other close; for a brief moment, the physical pain both women suffer fades away.

'I know what you're thinking,' Connie says, pointing to her injuries, 'but please don't worry about me.'

'I thought I recognised your voice but assumed it was a dream. I've been having plenty of vivid dreams recently. You'll stay, won't you? For as long as you'd like. You know this is your home as much as ours. We'll look after you. I know it would put Liam's mind at ease. He's been calling every day.'

'Kenny said as much.'

'Please, we'd love to have you. Let us take care of you. I'll call the doctor right now.'

For the first time since being released from prison, Connie feels like she belongs somewhere. 'I'm only saying a quick hello. I'm on my way west. A neighbour said I could stay at his holiday home until I come up with a plan. And I promise to see a doctor when I get there.'

Heather is unconvinced. 'Why haven't you called Liam yet? He's on to us day and night. Worried sick. Nobody knew about your early release. When we heard it on the news, Kenny went straight to Dublin but couldn't reach you because your phone was off. The staff at Mountjoy wouldn't give him any information. He walked around the area for hours, trying to spot you. Mary Elizabeth and Gerry are returning from Spain this weekend.'

'What are they doing that for?'

'You might not think so, but many people still love you and want to help you start again.'

'You all have your own problems to deal with.'

'And Liam?'

'I don't want to interrupt him with the World Cup only three months away. He mentioned he wasn't playing too well when we last spoke. I don't want to make things worse.'

'I imagine not knowing where you are isn't helping him much.'

'No, probably not.'

Heather holds Connie's hands tightly, just as she'd done with dozens of children over the decades. All around her are books, journals and encyclopaedias packed onto shelves, but Connie has always believed that Heather's wisdom came not from those pages but from real-life experiences.

'When we first began fostering almost forty-five years ago,' she begins, 'the social worker told us that loving a child was easy, but loving their behaviour was often not. "Do not define a child by how they act now. Instead, see their possibilities and help them realise their potential." The lady told us that our job was to see beyond their past and teach them how to open doors for themselves in the future.'

Heather looks deep into Connie's eyes.

'While your behaviour that night is not easy to love, I know the real you—caring, generous and sensitive, and the best mother imaginable. And I will never define you based on that night. Your work now is to forgive yourself and start living your life again. I know Jess would be the first to encourage you.'

Before Connie can consider this advice, she hears Abeo knocking on the kitchen window below.

'Who's that?' Heather asks, alarmed.

She kisses Heather. 'I love you and promise I'll be in touch soon. For now, you need to look after yourself. Please don't worry about me.'

Connie runs down the stairs, ignoring her body's pleas to slow down, and returns to the kitchen as Abeo enters.

'I apologise for barging in, but they're very close.'

'Wait,' Kenny says to Connie, recognising the man. 'Isn't that—?'

'I can't get the engine working,' Abeo interrupts, fighting to be heard over a van horn nearby.

'What's going on, Connie? You're frightening me.'

'They're after me. I foolishly returned to the village this morning, and they saw me.'

'And did that to you?'

Connie nods.

'And him? What's that thief got to do with all of this?'

'He's a good man, Kenny, I promise. God knows where I'd be if it weren't for him. I can't believe I've brought this trouble to your home. To you and Heather. But we had no choice. They followed us all the way here in their van, and then the car's engine started breaking down.'

'Don't worry about Heather and me—we are big and bold enough. And we have Prince to protect us.'

'They're dangerous people, Kenny, and they've every reason to be angry.'

'Well, they won't be nearly as angry as me if they come anywhere close to you again. You've paid for what happened that night. Giving you a beating will hardly bring the poor girl back, will it? Now, tell me, where are you going? Have you somewhere to stay?'

'There's a caravan park,' Abeo explains unenthusiastically. 'On the coast. It's isolated. But maybe she should stay here with you?'

'Absolutely,' Kenny says. 'You need your family around you. This caravan park doesn't sound great.'

'If we can get there, I'll be safe.'

Before Kenny can argue any further, the van horn sounds again.

'Is your car in view?' he asks Abeo, who shakes his head.

'I pushed it into one of those sheds. It's behind the turf.'

'Okay, good. You can take mine.'

'No!' Connie interjects. 'You need it. How's Heather going to get to physio?'

'We'll manage.'

'Do you still have your motorbike, Kenny?'

'I do, of course. It's in the shed.'

'Abeo, can you ride a motorbike?'

'Well, yes, but can you sit on one?'

'Don't worry about me.'

'I'll be able to bring it back later,' Abeo adds, in case Kenny needs any persuasion. He doesn't.

'I'll go out onto the road and distract them,' Kenny says, removing a key from a set. 'And you drive up the lane that runs alongside the bog. It will bring you onto the back road towards Athlone. Hopefully, unseen.'

'I'm so sorry for this trouble.'

Kenny waves his finger in front of her. 'Shush, that's what family is for, and Heather and I will always be your family. No matter what has happened or will happen. We love you. Remember that.'

'Thank you.'

A further commotion outside, close to the gate, interrupts their exchange.

'Quick! Get the bike from the garage,' he instructs Abeo, 'and Connie will direct you through the wood and onto the lane. It would probably be best to avoid turning on the engine until then. Go!'

CHAPTER EIGHTEEN
THEN, SATURDAY EVENING

ON CONNIE'S INSISTENCE, she and Bosco had just taken a series of photographs together in the booth, using the variety of costumes, wigs and props on offer. Observing the action from a distance, Mary Elizabeth couldn't believe Connie was dominating the flirtatious exchanges. She'd even cheered after spotting her usually timid pal sit on her date's lap while striking ridiculous poses.

While catching their breath on the lawn beside the ravaged piñata, Connie quizzed Bosco on his favourite subject. 'Which star do you like most?'

'Would you throw me out if I said you?'

'I most certainly would not, Bosco. I'm not the violent type.'

'You're probably used to men complimenting you.'

'It's almost boring at this stage.'

He rested his hand on hers. 'I'd say you could write a novel with all the chat-up lines you receive.'

'To be honest, I couldn't even write a limerick.'

'I find that hard to believe.'

'I find it hard to believe you know so much about the stars. You must have been fierce brainy in school.'

'My school achievements would even be shorter than your limerick. I've got an uncle who's an astronomer, and he shared his passion with me. We're the nerds in the family. It's cloudy now, but tonight, near Oldcastle, the view of the stars should be magnificent.'

'Magnificent?' she teased, adopting a dramatic voice.

'Magnificent. Just like—'

'Me?'

'You think a lot of yourself, don't you? I was going to say, "Magnificent, like this sangria!"'

'Oi!'

'Mary Elizabeth suggested earlier that you might like to see the "magnificent—just like sangria—stars" from there. We might even glimpse Connie Major if nature is on our side.'

'Mary Elizabeth's a great woman for making suggestions.'

'Well, if it means getting you all to myself, then the good woman won't be receiving any complaints from me!'

'I'd say your silver tongue has broken many hearts.'

'The only heart I've any interest in at the moment is—'

'Mine?'

'Is the one belonging to the person who made this magnificent sangria! Where are they so that I can declare my admiration?'

'You should come with a warning, you rogue! I know it's different from astronomy, but do you know anything about star signs? Not that I believe in all that nonsense. I'm a Libra—very indecisive, apparently.'

'Well, if you're bad at making decisions, Connie Maguire, let me help you: come with me to Oldcastle to watch the stars.' He checked his watch. 'You've about an hour to decide!'

As Bosco moved close to her to steal a kiss in the gathering dusk, Jess hesitantly approached them.

'Connie, sorry for butting in, but can I have a word with you?'

'Yes, of course. Bosco, give me a minute.'

'You can have sixty of them. Then, that hill in Oldcastle will need your answer!'

In her rush to stand up, Connie experienced a wave of nausea, which she overcame with deep breaths while Jess led her towards the side of the cottage.

'Is everything all right, my love?'

'Yes. No. Yes, it is. I think. It's Liam.'

'He came back with you, didn't he?'

'Yeah, but he insisted on calling his dad again before we arrived here. I tried to stop him.'

Connie suddenly felt a chill. Nick was determined to sabotage everyone's day.

'Liam didn't want to give out to him,' Jess continued, 'but to say how disappointed he was by his disappearance. Today of all days, you know?'

'Go on.'

'Well, he's in his bedroom now, in a funk. He seems to think you told his dad to leave. That he wasn't welcome in Liam's life.'

'What?' Connie was instantly reminded of how manipulative and vindictive Nick could be. 'We had an exchange, but suggesting I said he wasn't welcome in Liam's life is untrue.'

'I knew that, and I told Liam as much. I wouldn't worry about it, Connie. It's probably the excitement of the past few days, not helped by having one too many. And you know how he can throw himself into moods now and then.'

'Oh, I certainly do! I'll go into him and straighten things out.'

Connie wrapped her arms around Jess. How blessed her son was to have this grounding presence in his life. Earlier, Nick minimised their relationship as nothing more than a passing phase. 'I'll give it another week,' he had jeered. But Connie hoped the pair's relationship would benefit from Liam's change in fortunes. He wasn't like his father. Connie had reared him to respect women, but if there was a time when her son needed the stability of a loving relationship, it was now as he moved to the next level.

'I'll come and find you later,' Connie promised Jess before inhaling a pint of water; something told her she'd need her wits for this exchange with Liam.

* * *

Connie stepped over some guests huddled together in the narrow hallway, deep in the throes of gossip. One girl spoke ill of her crummy boyfriend; Connie empathised with her disdain. Today was supposed to be a day to remember for her family and friends, but Nick and his poisonous ways had ensured it would be memorable for all the wrong reasons. Following her interview with the journalist, she took an additional tablet to help elevate her mood. She counted three today, but no more after that.

She stopped outside Liam's door. Across it hung the many posters of rugby players he'd carefully cut out of magazines as a child. Over the years, Connie had wasted hours knee-deep in conflicting articles discussing the consequences of boys living in fatherless homes. Rightly or wrongly, they steered her to the belief that Liam's obsession with these rugby players and the game itself sprung from a need to compensate for Nick's absence.

'If being rugby-mad is the worst that happens, then things didn't turn out too badly for him,' her father would always say to comfort her.

He was right, but it hadn't made her feel better. Her anxieties were eased only by the help medication, first prescribed to her as a temporary treatment. After taking the first tablet, she felt a calmness that had eluded her all her life; the scramble in her mind finally vanished. The self-doubts, the worries, the self-loathing. In their place came a sudden change in form. Self-love and hope.

Pleas for her doctor to up her dose or provide refills had fallen on deaf ears. Instead, her doctor recommended alternative, natural approaches. She tried getting her supplies of Valium and Xanax online before 'doctor shopping' in the real world by obtaining prescriptions from multiple practitioners in multiple clinics. However, after catching her stealing his prescription notebook and stamp, her fourth doctor identified Connie's addiction. Her dark secrets soon unravelled.

With Liam and Mary Elizabeth's support and stints attending counselling sessions and regular meetings in Narcotics Anonymous, she had gradually but successfully weaned herself off all medication. Instead, she treated her anxiety with the alternative methods that had been first recommended to her: breathwork, CBT, yoga, hypnosis, nutrition, aromatherapy, teas and books. And many baths. However, the memory of how good prescription medication made her feel never went away.

Everything was fine until her father was diagnosed with dementia, and after a few months of heart-breaking care, Connie succumbed to the lure of medication again.

'I promise, my love, it's over now,' she had told Liam after he discovered the stash in her handbag. And on that occasion, she successfully kept her vow, pulling herself out of the brief relapse and ignoring the siren call of what lay hidden in her mattress.

Until today.

'Liam,' she called out, knocking on the door. 'Can I come in?'

'Of course,' he replied, his diction, like her own, rough around the edges. She found him lying on his bed, spinning a rugby ball on his finger.

'Taking some time out?' she asked. Boxes and suitcases, packed ahead of his move, lay scattered around the room.

'What did you say to Dad?' he questioned. When something was on his mind, he addressed it immediately.

'I believe Nick told you I wasn't very welcoming, but that wasn't the case.'

'Really?'

'Really. It wasn't a pleasant exchange—the word "schtick" was thrown about a few times—but this is your big day, and I know how much you wanted him to be here. I wouldn't do anything to jeopardise that. He's …' She searched for the right words. 'He's complicated. A perfectionist, you could say. He likes things to be a certain way.'

His way.

'I called him because I didn't want this anger inside me for the rest of the evening,' Liam explained, 'and let me tell you, I was angry. And then, after all that, I catch my future mother-in-law stealing the gifts we received from those companies.'

'Hold on a second—mother-in-law?'

'Did I say that?'

'Have you proposed?'

'Not yet. I wanted Dad to be there, so I rang him again. But he was annoyed that I was interrupting him. Him annoyed with me, even though he left without telling me!

Anyway, he said you threw him out and threatened to call the police if he ever tried to contact me again.'

'You don't believe him, do you?'

'Nah, I knew he was full of it. It was just …'

Connie waited for him to catch his thoughts.

'Disappointing. What I would have given for you two to be in a photograph with me earlier, along with Jess wearing the ring I bought her. I wished my dad was as excited about my life as everyone else.'

'Oh, I'm certain he is, but he has an unusual way of expressing himself.' Connie couldn't help defending him, if only for her son's sake.

'You'd find something positive to say about Donald Trump.'

'I would not, although orange skin will make a comeback one day, mark my words! My love, I hope you know that, deep down, your dad is immensely proud of you. We all are. Especially your old mammy.'

'Do you know what he got me as a present?' He reached for a book on the bedside locker, '*The Year in Politics.*'

'I see. Well, maybe Nick thought you might want to run for president after hanging up your rugby boots.'

'And inside the first page,' Liam continued, opening the book, "Happy Christmas, Barry. Up Fianna Fáil!" He gave me Uncle Barry's old Christmas present from someone called Gina O'Toole to congratulate me for finally making the Irish team. If nothing else, I suppose it'll make great kindling if my new apartment gets cold this winter. Or maybe Breege can flog it on her website.'

Connie lay down beside him. 'Try not to be upset.'

'I'm just feeling sorry for myself. But I know what will put a smile on my face.'

He handed her the rugby ball. 'You've got to spin it on your finger for ten seconds, unaided. And if you succeed, I'll score a try in the first match of the next World Cup! And if you don't—'

'Not another word! I've been blamed for enough today without being responsible for ruining your career as well.'

'You taught me how to do this trick! And if you don't hit the ten-second mark, you won't get your birthday present.'

'What? You already gave me roses and our photo. Our gorgeous photo. You shouldn't have gotten me anything.'

'You won't get anything if you don't manage ten seconds. All you'll get is a second-hand book about Irish politics!'

After the laughter died down, Connie placed the ball on her fingers and, surprisingly, successfully spun it, initially using her other hand for support. After building up speed and momentum, she released her second hand.

'One, two, three.'

'Oi! You're counting too quickly, Mam!'

'Six, seven, eight.'

Liam tried to blow the ball from her finger with mock force.

'Nine and ten! Wahoo!' Connie roared. 'I've not lost it! A champion never does!'

'Okay, okay, Champ! Now for your present. I think you've deserved it at this stage. Close your eyes.' He led her to the window and pulled the net curtain to one side. 'The paperwork is sorted, and all you have to do is turn the key.'

Connie's eyes shot open. A Mini Cooper stood on the driveway with a red ribbon on the roof.

'My rugby contract is signed, sealed and delivered, and there was only one way I wanted to spend my first cheque. On my favourite girl in the world!'

'There's no way your first cheque covered the cost of that.'

'I'd savings, and it's part-financed. I know there were problems with you driving in the past, but I want you to know how proud I am of you for overcoming your addiction.'

'Oh, that's so lovely of you,' she said, her cheeks colouring, 'but there's something I need to tell you.'

'And it can wait 'til later. I want us to sit in the car and get a feel for it!'

Connie's heart was fit to somersault from her chest. They skipped through the cottage and into the front garden, the other curious guests following them. She played along with the surprise, but there was no way she could keep it.

She would also come clean about her relapse—*my one-day relapse*. Connie was determined that this new decade wouldn't be full of secrets and lies.

'I love the reg!' one guest shouted. Connie had to re-read the letters several times to make sense of it: 'MAMMY MAGUIRE'.

'Hop in!' Liam ordered, holding the door open for her and dramatically circling his hand like a fairy-tale prince.

Connie slid into the front seat and beeped the car horn, much to the delight of the guests, already sharing images and footage of the unveiling on social media. She noticed Liam's expression beside her. At that moment, she'd never seen him so proud. The car would have to be returned to the dealer in the morning.

For now, where's the harm in pretending?

CHAPTER NINETEEN

NOW

CONNIE HAD TRAVELLED extensively throughout Ireland on several rugby team buses, but this desolate region of north Connaught isn't familiar to her. She maintains her tight grip around Abeo's waist as they close in on their destination; the distinctive smell and spirit of the Atlantic Ocean are becoming more omnipotent with every passing moment. Gulls, squawking overhead, herald its imminent unveiling.

Uprooting to the opposite side of the country has precedent amongst Connie's family. How often did her late mother abandon domestic responsibilities to visit Lough Derg in County Donegal? There, she would take part in lengthy pilgrimages to repent for the sins committed by those orbiting her world, namely her daughter.

'For all the good it does you,' her mother once spat before boarding the bus.

Connie becomes distracted, noticing glimmers of light sparkling on the road ahead. After they clear a low bridge, she suspects they've driven over shards of glass; when the motorbike's front wheel deflates, she knows for certain. They pull over and remove their helmets, a challenging task for Connie.

'I don't think Kenny has driven this bike in a while.' Her voice sounds tired and raspy.

'It explains why the tyre punctured so easily.' Abeo scans their surroundings, his frustration clear in every laboured breath. 'Although speeding across the country probably didn't help.'

Connie imagines one of the many reasons Abeo has misgivings about this impromptu expedition is now revealing itself: isolation. Given the late hour, it could be a while before help arrives.

'You wait here,' he instructs, noticing a house five hundred metres in front of them. 'Maybe I can convince someone to give us a lift to the petrol station. There's one between here and the caravan park. I'd say it's only about ten minutes away.' He looks at his watch, heading off. 'It should still be open if I can get them to bring us there quickly.'

Alone, Connie ventures across the narrow road, where a thicket of reeds blows in the evening breeze. She envies their freedom of movement and wonders how long it will take to have a whisper of their fluidity again. Inspired, she attempts to stretch her arms. Sitting on a stone wall, Liam weaves a bracelet from blades of grass.

'Do you remember that time—'

'Stop! I know what you're going to say, Mam! Don't remind me!'

'When you went on that school tour to Connemara and thought you'd put on sun lotion when it was cheap cream I'd gotten for my cracked heels.'

Liam groans at the memory. 'I couldn't leave the house for a week. The peeling! The pain!'

'I'm sure everybody thought I was the worst mother in the world.'

'Nobody thought that, certainly not me.' He places the bracelet around her thin wrist. 'If there were awards ...'

'I'd need a mantelpiece!'

He examines the congealed blood under the bandages on her hands.

'I'll be fine. There's no need to worry about your poor mammy.'

'Funny you should mention being "poor". You better start using that money I've deposited into your account.'

'That's your money.'

'That's *our* money.'

'I'll be fine with what I have.'

'Depriving yourself of the basics like food and proper accommodation won't bring Jess back, you know? You had to escape the village quickly this afternoon, but it's not too late to book yourself into a hotel. Or come to Portugal. Fly out of Knock Airport in the morning. I can rent us a house away from the other lads. It would be you and me, no one else. Like the old times. Please.'

'I don't want to interrupt you, Liam. You need to focus on the World Cup.'

'Yes, so you've mentioned.'

'Imagine if those reporters or Breege found out I was sunning myself in Portugal in some fancy mansion. You can be certain they'd hate me even more than they do already.'

'Okay, okay.' Liam smiles, attempting to lift her spirits. 'Let's forget about people who hate you and focus on those who don't.'

'Kenny! Thanks for reminding me—I need to call him.'

On the journey here, the thoughts of bringing harm to the two people she loves more than anyone, Liam aside, proved so overwhelming it took everything in her power not to vomit on the back of the motorcycle. Fleeing Kenny and Heather's house meant she had to hide her battered handbag under her coat. She retrieves it and turns the phone on for the first time since leaving prison. It pings with an assault of messages and notifications. She doesn't want to read or listen to any of them. While trying to call Kenny, she accidentally opens the most recent message:

'We know where u are. U won't escape 4 long!'

'Don't worry, Mam. They're all talk,' Liam assures her. 'They've got no idea where you're going.'

'What if Simon told them?'

'Why would he? It was his idea for you to hide out in his caravan park. Besides, he'd hardly want those hooligans anywhere near the place. They haven't a clue where you are, I promise you. In saying that, if you're not coming to Portugal, I think you should return to—'

'That's who I was trying to call.'

Nervously, she dials Kenny's number.

'Hello,' she says into the phone when he finally picks up. 'Are you okay?'

Not only did Kenny diffuse the situation with Jess' family, but he reveals that their car is road-worthy again, lifting a weight off Connie's bruised shoulders.

'Abeo seems like a reformed man,' Kenny praises. 'Your father's instinct was right.'

'I'm sorry for bringing so much danger.'

'Connie, your father and I used to be known as the Terrible Twosome back in the day. We were feared from Timbuktu to Kathmandu! Those lads had no idea who they were messing with!'

'That's why I want you to stay with Kenny,' Liam cuts in. 'He'll protect you—no better man. You know it's what Granddad would have wanted.'

'Tell me, Kenny,' Connie says. 'Did Dad know what happened that night? Do you think it's why he died so soon after?'

'No, Connie, I assure you. He didn't have a clue. We made sure of that. Even if he did, that man would have loved you all the same.'

After promising to keep in touch, Connie hangs up.

'Have you thought about what you'll do with your days in the caravan park?' Liam asks. 'I hope it's busier than here, only two houses within miles around.'

'Two?' she asks before noticing a bungalow hidden behind trees. She turns towards Abeo, who remains far from the first house.

'Do you think I should call into this other house and see if they can help us?'

'Your friend seems to have things under control.'

After some hemming and hawing, Connie abandons the main road and ventures down the narrow lane towards the house, her slight frame dwarfed by the mountains behind her. She stops along the way, leaning against the wall that divides the many fields to allow a moment of drowsiness to pass.

'Mam, this isn't a good idea.'

'Maybe you're right,' she agrees, already feeling the physical toll of her short walk here.

'Are you talking to yourself?' A tall man with a jolly voice stands by the front door, his ill-fitting trousers held up by braces. 'I do it myself all the time. We can get help for that, I'm told.'

'Actually, I am looking for help,' Connie replies. 'For something different, though. We've had a puncture.'

The man saunters down the driveway with a pronounced limp. 'I'm sorry to hear that. I'll take a guess and say that there was glass on the road. Don't expect to see the council cleaning it up anytime soon.'

He opens the gate, but Connie hesitates. 'I don't want to bother you,' she says. 'My friend is up at another house across the road, and I'm sure they're already waiting for me to give us a lift to the petrol station.'

'The Murtaghs? Across the road? Sure, they've been dead for five years, may they rest in peace. You won't be getting any lifts from them unless you plan to hitch a lift on their angel wings, God be good to them.' His hearty chuckle makes Connie smile. 'Here, on the other hand, we've hundreds of tyres in all shapes and sizes. I'm a mechanic, you see.'

'Are you?'

'What's your name?'

'Connie,' she answers, immediately kicking herself for revealing her identity.

'I'm Jimmy Junior. Connie is the short for Concepta, isn't it? A friend of mine was a nurse in the regional hospital in Castlebar. His aunt worked there as well. Sure, no wonder they're all as fit as fiddles in that family. But my friend used to call her Aunty Cepty, which sounds like anti-septic—confusing in a hospital, as you can imagine. So, they settled on Connie. You could probably do with a trip to the hospital yourself, no offence. You get in a fight?'

'Something like that.'

'I hope you gave as good as you got. Come on in. If you don't catch your death from all your cuts and bruises, it'll be from pneumonia.'

Connie follows the man towards the back of the bungalow.

'You've got a husky voice,' he says. 'It's like that one from the pictures. I saw her in the cinema once in

Castlebar. Now, that's going back years. What's her name again?'

'It will come to you, I'm sure.'

'I wouldn't bank on it because my memory isn't what it used to be. Did you ever fancy being on the big screen like Kim Basinger or Bo Derek? Now that I think of it, maybe you could play Rambo or Rocky with all those cuts!'

Liam stands in front of her. 'Mam, please turn back and pretend you see Abeo.'

The man opens the side door. 'Come on in, and you'll meet my cousin.'

CHAPTER TWENTY
THEN, SATURDAY NIGHT

THE PUBLIC RESPONSE to the guests' videos and images on social media was phenomenal. Even those prone to begrudgery held their whisht. Liam claimed an impressive quarter of a million followers across various platforms, meaning the birthday girl received messages from rugby fans worldwide in myriad languages.

The video generating the most traction showed mother and son sitting proudly together in her new Mini Cooper. Charmed users had remixed the footage with The Spice Girls' 'Mama' and Bette Midler's 'Wind Beneath My Wings'. #Connie40 was trending in Ireland. The only place people wanted to be that night was in a garden in north County Meath. Judging by the sudden upsurge in guests, many felt personal invitations were unnecessary.

For the first time in her life, Connie basked in the spotlight. Rather than rebuking people for taking her photograph or pleading with them to avoid her 'bingo wings' or 'double chin', she was happy to strike a pose or film messages of gratitude.

'Forty is the new twenty-one!' she gushed. 'Repeat my mantra after me, everyone: new beginnings!'

She wasn't the only person seduced by the attention. Liam's friends were desperate to keep up the momentum online and insisted on filming more videos with ideas ranging from drinking games to charades, spin the bottle and 'let's remove our shirts and jump off the thatched roof and into the bushes!'

The latest idea was more acceptable and less life-threatening: dancing the Cha Cha around Connie's new car. Mary Elizabeth gamely led the troupe as they attempted the simple movements. With the number of guests mushrooming with every moment, the line of dancers soon spanned the entire lane. Even Connie, who usually avoided the dancefloor, readily joined in and showcased impressive footwork.

New beginnings.

'One, two, cha, cha, cha; one, two, cha, cha, cha,' Mary Elizabeth roared, 'anyone not giving their all will be flogged with the piñata stick!'

'Don't make promises you can't keep!' Andy joked.

Liam sat on the window ledge, his arms draped over Jess, smiling.

As the routine ended, Connie broke away to catch her breath. And to steady her mind. Over the past hour, she had received not only the keys to a Mini Cooper but also an assault of celebratory drinks. Yes, the day had gotten off to a shaky start, and there were indiscretions and unfortunate encounters along the way, but this party had blossomed into one of the happiest days of her life. And, she had reasoned, the best way to prolong this unfamiliar elation was by drinking. Now, her queasy stomach and spinning head were letting her know the errors of her ways. She leaned against the door and took a series of inhalations.

'One, two, cha, cha, cha,' she repeated, finding the hypnotic rhythm helpful. No sooner had the wave of nausea passed than a hand landed on her shoulder.

'We didn't make it to Oldcastle, Connie Major, but that doesn't mean I'm allowing our date to end.'

She turned around to find Bosco and his bushy beard standing in front of her.

'Is that so?' Connie hoped she sounded seductive. Her imprecise diction didn't faze her admirer, who promptly kissed her. It had been so long since her last embrace that Connie wondered whether she was kissing him properly. When his hands moved up her back, she knew Bosco was at least invested in the moment, regardless of her ability. And so was she. Flashbacks of her first kiss with the father of her child attempted to bully their way into her mind. They failed. Connie, with her birthday mantra, made sure of it.

Raucous cheers soon disrupted her romantic interlude. Connie ignored them and draped her arms around Bosco for another, longer kiss.

It's my party, and I'll smooch if I want to!

* * *

As sure as the sun sets in the west, Irish gatherings descend into high-spirited singsongs, and Connie and Liam's party was no different. Under the fairy lights and accompanied by some reasonably in-tune guitar playing from Andy, the birthday girl and Breege belted out her party piece, 'The Black Velvet Band'. What the women lacked in melody, they made up for in intensity, and on reaching the chorus, Connie instructed everyone to join in. Not caring to share the limelight, Breege held the last note for what seemed like an eternity to some of her less enthusiastic audience. As she milked the moment, Liam assisted his mother back towards her chair, which was no easy task, even for an athlete.

'I don't know who this diva is,' he said, handing her water, 'but I hope you'll return my mother to me in the morning, please!'

'New beginnings!' Connie hiccupped. 'New beginnings!'

She sipped the water and held onto her chair to steady herself.

'Mary Elizabeth, keep an eye on Mam, will you?' Liam said as he walked towards the kitchen. 'Jess, are you ready?'

'It seems like you've hit it off with your date, huh?' Mary Elizabeth whispered mischievously into her best friend's ear. Under a bunch of balloons, Bosco chatted to monosyllabic Rory, but he couldn't keep his eyes off Connie.

'Thanks to him and your matchmaking skills, Connie Major is up amongst the stars, moon and galaxies.'

She tried to look towards the sky but almost fell off the chair. Mary Elizabeth grabbed her by the arm just in time to keep her upright.

'Look what your son's girlfriend has baked for you.' Mary Elizabeth pointed towards Jess, carrying a cake into the garden, candles flickering on top. Liam and the other guests sang 'Happy Birthday'.

'What's happening, Mary Elizabeth?' Connie whispered. 'I bought Liam a gorgeous cake from Gerry. Let me just—'

'And we'll get to it later,' Mary Elizabeth said in a noticeably pointed tone. 'Sweetie, I hope you haven't …'

'Haven't?'

'Nothing. I know you wouldn't do anything so stupid. I'm going to get you some coffee in a minute. It's been a long day for everyone.'

Liam positioned the cake on the table beside Connie while 'and so say all of us' reverberated around the garden.

'With that many candles, I hope someone has the fire brigade on standby!' Breege teased as she used the flames to light a cigarette.

When 'hip-hip-hooray' made way for calls to 'make a wish', Connie looked at her star.

My wish is to keep you all safe. Especially my champion, Liam, and his gorgeous Jess. New beginnings for us all.

With help from Liam and Mary Elizabeth, she blew out every candle. Determined to steal or at least sully the moment, Breege lost her balance, nearly knocking over the cake, but Liam managed to save the day with his famous quick reflexes. Not that the near-miss accident bothered Breege in the slightest.

'The lungs on you, Connie,' she praised, leading another round of applause.

Connie accepted another glass of cava, ignoring a frown from Mary Elizabeth. 'That's the power of yoga! You should all start joining me! Even that journalist today was impressed by my ... by me. By moi!'

'Sure, I won't be blowing out forty candles for another twenty years!' Mary Elizabeth quipped, removing the drink from Connie's hand.

Liam held his glass aloft. 'A toast to my mother, my best friend. I saw a meme the other day that said something along the lines of, "Like a compass, you've guided me every step of the way", and I instantly thought of you. Mam, I would well and truly be lost without you—I *will* be lost without you from next week on!'

'I hope your game is better than your speeches,' Breege roared. 'I can only imagine what you'll come out with on your wedding day.'

'It's funny that you should mention weddings,' Liam continued, bending a knee towards Jess, eliciting a collective gasp from the guests. 'I know there has already been a lot of excitement over the past few hours, but I want to ask you something.'

He held a breathtaking diamond ring in front of Jess, who had to wipe away her tears to see it.

'I hope you know how much I adore you. I've no idea what the future holds, but one thing is for sure: I want you by my side. So, will you do me the honour of marrying me?'

'Yes, yes, yes!' Jess shouted. 'Yes!'

As they kissed to a roar of applause, Connie turned to Mary Elizabeth. 'Why is she saying "yes"? What has happened?'

'Your son is getting married, that's what's happened! There's going to be a wedding!'

'A wedding? I can't believe it!' Connie struggled to her feet and hugged the lovebirds tightly. 'Guys, I'm over the … What do you call it, Bosco? My personal astrologer.'

'Astronomer,' he corrected with a smile. 'And it's "over the moon".'

'Over the moon! Thank you! I'm over the moon!'

CHAPTER TWENTY-ONE

NOW

'I DIDN'T REALISE we were expecting company.'

'So make sure you're on your best behaviour, Dennis,' Jimmy Junior teases, swatting his cousin's feet from the kitchen table. 'It's not often we've ladies in the house.'

As Dennis jumps up and grabs two enamel mugs from a shelf, Connie keeps a hand on the door handle. Behind his bumble-bee-coloured glasses, she notices his right eye suffers a squint.

'Are you going to introduce us, Jimbob, or should I pluck a name out of the sky? I'm thinking she could be a Rita. Or a Susan.'

'This is Connie,' Jimmy Junior informs him.

'You had a fall?' Dennis asks, fishing a bottle of whiskey from a cupboard. 'This should help the pain.'

The two men invite her to sit in an armchair in the kitchen corner. When Connie reluctantly complies, her hosts tower over her, the ineffective springs lowering her almost to floor level. Dennis sits on the arm of the chair, ramrod straight, and pours her a generous measure of whiskey.

'To better days,' he says, referencing her cuts and bruises.

'To better days,' she replies, without drinking.

'Your voice is familiar, Connie. Are you on the radio?'

'It is, isn't it, cousin? I was thinking of that actress in the cinema. She was in the film set in the jungle with your man and the little fella.'

'Kathleen Turner.'

'Kathleen Turner. That's exactly it. You never get that before, Connie?'

'I haven't,' she replies, relieved that they aren't discussing the familiarity of her face. 'Jimmy Junior, you mentioned you've some tyres for a motorcycle? I'll pay.'

Dennis sighs and after returning to the table, turns on the television. 'Don't think me rude, Connie, but there's a programme about the rugby lads in a minute. I've been looking forward to it all week.'

'The Irish team?' Connie asks. In the wardrobe back in her former home, there was a box bursting with magazine and newspaper cut-outs, along with videos and DVDs of Liam's various interviews. Every snippet of coverage thrilled her, from the local to international media. Little did she realise that one day, she would steal the spotlight from her son by becoming the focus of the articles and headlines.

Dennis flicks through the channels. 'It's been on the ads all week. Exclusive interviews and behind-the-scenes footage. If you didn't know about it, you're not much of a fan, are you?'

'No, I suppose not.' Connie realises it is time to leave. With some difficulty, given the shabbiness of the chair, she rises and makes her way to the door. 'Sorry for barging in on you, and thanks for the—'

Jimmy Junior follows her and wedges himself between Connie and the door. His earlier jolly demeanour has abandoned him entirely. 'We were getting to know each other. What about your tyre? I don't take cash or cards, though. How else can you pay me?'

Connie's throat tightens. 'But what did you expect would happen by coming in here?' she imagines Liam screaming at her.

Dennis doubles over in laughter, excitedly slapping his hand against the table's surface. The sudden gesture causes a plate of butter to crash to the floor.

'Show us a little something, Connie,' Jimmy Junior whispers.

She attempts to pull the handle, but he immediately shuts the door before leaning against it.

'I don't know about you, Dennis, but I feel our guest is very ungrateful. First, she barely touched our whiskey, and now she won't give us a little peepshow! Two bachelor men—be charitable.'

'Ah, leave her alone, Jimbob,' his cousin finally orders, tiring of the tomfoolery.

The fear Connie initially felt gives way to anger. Twenty-one months of anger. That morning, she had begged Breege to treat her like a punching bag because the thumping and kicking and slapping were more palatable than those devastating words and recriminations. This savage, who thinks women can be plied with cheap alcohol and assaulted, would not be offered the same opportunity.

A water pipe suddenly begins creaking furiously somewhere in the kitchenette area.

'Not again!'

'Mam, run! Now!' Liam shouts, appearing beside her.

But Connie isn't prepared to run just yet. As Jimmy Junior turns towards the faulty sink, she takes advantage of the distraction and shoves him into the display cabinet slumped against the wall. His piercing screams drown out the sound of the smashing glass.

'Don't you *ever* do that to another woman again,' Connie roars, 'you pervert!'

Dennis grabs a pair of scissors from the counter, but Connie deftly swipes it from his hand and forces it against his throat.

'Mam! Stop! Just get out of here! I'm begging you!'

Connie suddenly drops the scissors from her trembling hands.

What am I doing?

After opening the door, she hurries to the front gate but catches her finger on the rusty latch. Ignoring the sharp pain, she jumps over it instead, falling onto the cattle grid. Behind her, Jimmy Junior scrambles down the driveway, but he's too slow and breathless and can only look on as Connie disappears up the lane.

CHAPTER TWENTY-TWO
THEN, SATURDAY NIGHT

CONNIE ATTEMPTED TO gain control of her actions, but her body and mind were no longer working in tandem. Mary Elizabeth had instructed her to sit at the kitchen table only moments earlier. She clearly remembered the kettle reaching its boil, battling to be heard over the singing in the garden. Now, somehow, she was standing in her bedroom, removing her dress and replacing it with pyjamas. She wobbled and grabbed the shelf beside the door, knocking a collection of books to the floor.

Abandoning her pyjama bottoms—or were they yoga leggings?—she stumbled over the mess and returned to the hallway. Unfamiliar guests hugged her. Or were they trying to hold her up?

'Yes,' Connie replied to someone, but what was the question? Or was there even a question in the first place? 'I don't want toast. Yes, I do.'

Who had offered her toast? Was Mary Elizabeth still making her coffee?

There's Liam.

Connie was unsure if she was looking at her son in front of her or in the photograph. Yes, there was a framed photograph in her hand—jewels sparkled around its edges, like the necklace Teddy had given her. Holding the image close, she whispered, 'I love you.'

'And I love you, too—now, let go of me before I choke!' *Who said that?*

'I'm putting you to bed in a minute, Mam, so eat your toast.'

There was another crash somewhere, followed by loud and angry screams. In the garden, people were cursing.

'Breege! I need you to stand up!'

That's Liam again. She looked towards the mayhem. *Why is Breege destroying the photo booth?*

The screaming from the garden grew louder; she could hear Mary Elizabeth's voice. Andy kept shouting, 'Don't you touch my sister!' Then Gerry said, 'Don't you touch *my* sister'—emphasis was on the 'my'. She could hear Jess repeat 'Mam' over and over.

Someone was pulling down the fairy lights, or was she confusing the glimmers of light with the crystals scattered around her cherished photograph? Or Teddy's necklace, maybe?

'Breege! You need to calm down!'

Should I help? Does Breege want toast?

Connie stepped into the garden. Where were all the guests? At least one hundred people sang 'Happy Birthday' to her an hour earlier. Now, there were only about twenty.

Maybe they were in the house, getting toast. She could make out a mobile phone being held aloft. Was the person filming what Breege was doing? Was it going to be uploaded to social media like all the other footage earlier in the party? Was the world going to see how the party had descended into chaos?

Our dirty secrets.

She swiped the phone and hurled it into the bush. Ignoring the guest's complaints—'What the hell did you do that for?'—Connie fled her party and the growing chaos.

Cool air, that's nice, she thought, walking towards the front of the cottage and passing her shiny birthday present. She toyed with the ribbon on the roof, remembering fielding messages from envious neighbours and former friends who'd learned about the new car through Liam's socials.

Something cracked under her foot: her ceramic flowerpots. Had she just broken them, or were they already smashed? Did Liam mention something about damaging them earlier that day? Why was he angry? Nick had done something to upset him. Her mouth suddenly felt dry, so she ventured towards the fountain in the village square.

To refresh myself.

However, she stumbled and fell before reaching the end of the lane. While examining her injured knees, Connie realised she was no longer wearing her maxi dress, and her legs were bare.

Didn't I change into my pyjamas? Where have they gone?

The fountain was now in front of her. Connie felt confused. Wasn't she sitting on the lane, nursing her bloodied knee? There were objects sparkling in her line of vision. Was it Teddy's necklace again, she wondered, or the framed photograph? Or the fairy lights?

It's the coins at the bottom of the fountain.

She leaned forward, mesmerised by the hundreds of wishes scattered across the base, made by locals and tourists alike. Her nose touched the cool surface, then her entire body was submerged in the shallow water. She struggled to breathe.

Was I thrown in?

When she finally resurfaced and allowed a fit of coughing to pass, she made out a silhouette. A man. Her son? A rescuer? But why would her rescuer laugh at her and call her a 'bitch' and a 'fat slag'?

She watched the man cross the bridge, laughing and eating chips. An empty ketchup sachet fell from the crown of her head onto her nose, where it stuck. The person who'd pushed her into the fountain was the person she'd stood up to earlier for the first time in her life.

Nick. I need to get sick.

* * *

'Mam! Mam! You need to open the door now, or I will break it down!'

Liam and Jess, along with Mary Elizabeth, sporting a bloodied lip courtesy of Breege, bunched into the hallway.

After the drama had finally ended, Gerry brought the remaining guests and their many cameras to The Steeples. Only then did Liam realise that his mother was comatose inside the locked bathroom.

'Jess, will you put the kettle on?' Mary Elizabeth asked. 'I think we're all going to need a strong coffee.'

She turned to Liam. 'What are we going to do? Break the door down? Smash the window? I can hear her snoring, which is good—she's alive!—but I'd be worried she'd choke on her vomit.'

'I can't believe I'm asking this, but do you think she relapsed?'

Connie falling back on her old ways would explain how relaxed she had seemed that afternoon. Mary Elizabeth had expected her best friend to be on tenterhooks given the occasion and Nick's sudden return. But she wasn't, quite the opposite. Mary Elizabeth could kick herself for not being more sensitive during their exchange in the café.

'It could just be all the bubbles getting the better of her, Liam. God knows how much alcohol she had. How much we all had. But, yes, I think she took something. And before you get upset, I can assure you—'

'Mam! We need you to wake up!' Liam shouted again, taking his frustrations out on the door. It wasn't the first time he had thumped it. When Nick had once ignored several phone calls, young Liam channelled his frustration into the first thing he saw: the bathroom door. Stitches and a scolding from Connie followed, even though she understood his distress. With his anger now bubbling towards the surface, Liam could barely resist punching the door again. This was not how he had envisioned the day ending. How had he not noticed the signs earlier? 'The bath!' she had repeatedly said when everyone commented on how relaxed she seemed.

Was that what she had wanted to admit to him earlier in his bedroom? He hadn't given her the opportunity, too excited about revealing her birthday present. Apart from his granddad, Mary Elizabeth and the various doctors, nobody in the community knew about his mother's struggles, although Liam had always suspected their neighbours must have questioned her behaviour over the years. Slurring her words. The grogginess. The unsteady walking. The absent-mindedness. The poor concentration.

During those challenging times, his biggest fear had been that something would happen to a child in school, and his mother wouldn't have the wits to prevent it. Or worse, that she'd be the cause of it. The only crime she could ever be accused of was making terrible jokes, and he'd been determined it would stay that way.

Liam insisted that Connie receive expert help and address the toxic relationship with her mother, or 'Granny, the God-fearing Grump', as he'd referred to her. He was proud of Connie's initial willingness to overcome her many struggles. And, apart from a brief relapse three years earlier, he'd believed her demons were in the past. He'd even bought her the car to celebrate how far she'd come. As he pounded on the door again, Liam realised how naïve he'd been.

'Can you explain it to me, Mary Elizabeth, why would she do this? After everything we've been through together. Today was supposed to be her big day—*our* big day. Why couldn't she enjoy herself? What could she have been so anxious about? The only thing she had to do was cut some bloody cake!'

'I know you're angry, sweetie, but that's not how anxiety works,' Mary Elizabeth replied. 'There are times when your gorgeous mother can take on the world. And then there are other times she'd break out in a sweat in Tesco, deciding which pesto to buy. She'd think, "If I can't choose between the green or red jar, how can I make any proper life choices?" and then spiral into a tortuous, self-loathing inner monologue. It's a nasty, nasty condition, and when you don't suffer from it, it's easy to diminish and ridicule these experiences, but it's very real.'

'I never ridiculed them.'

'I don't mean you or anyone specifically. Just the world at large. These unreasonable thoughts suddenly take flight in her mind, sometimes without her awareness, and they refuse to budge. She obviously convinced herself that she needed a little support today.'

'And that's what we're here for, surely. Besides, where did these tablets come from? Does she have a stash hidden in the back of her wardrobe? How often does she take them? For God's sake, Mary Elizabeth, I can't believe we're back here again.'

Liam knew that alcohol combined with prescription medication was a recipe for disaster, and not even the shiftiest, back-alley doctor would recommend mixing the two. He had to open this door.

'Mam! Wake up!'

As he was about to kick the door down, a faint groan sounded inside the bathroom.

'Mam! Mam! Open up! You've no idea how much trouble you're in!' Liam gave another bang to the door to punctuate his point. 'What am I going to do now, Mary Elizabeth? I can't disappear to Dublin, and God knows where else for training camps if she's popping bloody pills again.'

'You can and you will,' Mary Elizabeth firmly replied, touching his troubled face. 'This is nothing more than a blip, and we'll address it head-on. There's no way we'll allow her to return to those dark days.'

Another louder groan sounded from the bathroom.

'Mam!'

A wet Connie eventually opened the door. Her smudged makeup made her look like a character from a horror film. For Liam, however, the scene was very much real.

'Let's get you to bed.'

'Go on with the others to The Steeples, Liam,' Mary Elizabeth said over the loud snores while exchanging Connie's sodden clothes for a dry t-shirt. 'It's only half ten. I'll stay here and look after her.'

'Thanks, but I've lost my mojo. You go on and bring Jess. I don't want her seeing Mam like this. She looks up to her, and I'd like to keep it that way.'

Mary Elizabeth kissed him on the forehead. 'We'll nip this in the bud.'

Alone, Liam rubbed his mother gently to drive the chill from her bones. Like the garden, her bedroom resembled a warzone, with books and clothes scattered across the floor. He had often found refuge here, but the comfort he once received simply from being around her belongings—her smell, her energy, her spirit—was now shattered, knowing that her dirty little secret was skulking here somewhere.

CHAPTER TWENTY-THREE

NOW

CONNIE SITS IN the van between Abeo and an *undead* Murtagh; the motorcycle and its defective tyre are in the back. The man's anecdotes about his job as a roofer are lighthearted, although she contributes little to the conversation.

Arriving at the petrol station, she spots a flashing neon sign outside and imagines it should read 'Joyce', but only the word 'Joy' is visible thanks to a couple of idle light bulbs. One of her many well-thumbed self-help books would suggest it was a sign from the universe.

Refusing Connie's offers of help, the two men take care of the motorcycle. While waiting, Connie joins an unimpressed Liam, throwing pebbles at an empty can.

'Your visit to that house wasn't your best idea, Mam.'

'I won't argue with you.'

'I don't like you being here. This isn't your patch—you don't know the people, and they don't know you. If ever there was a time when you needed your wits about you, it's now. What if that pervert hadn't been distracted by his sink? What if that waitress hadn't held Andy back this morning? Or Teddy hadn't chased away those vermin in the graveyard? Or Abeo hadn't saved you from Breege or Kenny from those bastards in the van? Do you see the pattern?'

Connie breaks away from Liam; even when he's a figment of her imagination, he manages to whip up strong emotions within her.

'Why on earth did you go into that house just now?' he continues. 'Since you woke up this morning, you've been making one bad decision after the other.'

'Well, they're my bad decisions to make.'

Her phone rings in her pocket. Liam, the real Liam, is calling her. After ignoring it, a notification informs her she has missed twenty-two calls from him.

'If only you'd answer the phone and let me get you on a flight to Portugal. You must listen to Heather: we can't change the past.'

'But we can change the subject, can't we?'

Like those occasions in his youth when he didn't receive the outcome he wanted, her son disappears. Without Liam to hold her accountable for her behaviour, she notices a man sitting beside a beautifully decorated wooden caravan on the far side of the petrol station. In front of him, a plastic table props up a sign: 'Tarot Readings'.

Despite his seated position and tall, spikey blonde hair, Connie realises he is short, and if it weren't for the wrinkles on his forehead, she might mistake him for a boy. Behind him, a woman feeds a horse.

'Are you looking for a reading?' the man asks, removing a pack of cards from his denim jacket. 'The cards will tell you what your future holds.'

Mary Elizabeth once dragged Connie to a psychic, who promptly showed her the exit. 'Come back when your heart and mind are open!'

'I don't think so,' she now replies.

'Then, pick a single card and allow it to guide you. And don't give me any money. Just keep my family in your prayers.'

'We all need a little direction now and then,' the woman encourages behind them.

Connie selects a card from near the top and is immediately surprised by its warmth. Holding it, she feels entrusted with the hopes and dreams of those who had previously chosen it. The feeling fortifies her: she isn't alone.

'Take a good look at it,' the man instructs.

Examining the striking image, Connie makes out a cloud with a hand emerging from it. This hand clasps onto a shaft, which sprouts leaves. In the distance stands a castle.

'The Ace of Wands,' the man reveals, without inspecting the card.

'What does it mean?'

'Is it facing up or down?'

'Up.'

'You'll have a breakthrough moment. The leaves on the wand mean growth, and do you see the castle? There will be opportunities opening up for you shortly. A new project, maybe. Even love. New beginnings.'

New beginnings.

'So, you think there's a future for me?'

The man smiles at Connie. 'So long you're open to it.'

Distracted by what's being said, Connie doesn't initially hear Abeo calling her name. She returns the card. 'You don't realise how much I needed to hear that.'

'I do,' the tarot reader assures her. 'And by the way, she's looking after you.'

'Who?'

Instead of answering, he disappears into the caravan.

She's looking after you, Connie repeats, walking the short distance towards the petrol station.

'I'll get some things,' Abeo says. 'Is there anything you need?'

She needs a long list of things, seeing as she came to the village nearly empty-handed, but toothpaste is all she can suggest. 'Let me give you some money.'

Abeo dismisses this suggestion. Connie wraps her scarf around her head and puts the sunglasses on her face. Like her body and the sign outside, the surprisingly busy store has seen better days. Displays lie empty with muck and dust littering the floor. As Abeo searches the shelves, a hand taps Connie's leg.

'What happened to your face?' a girl asks, her pink dress perfectly complementing her sweet voice.

A friend pinches her, clearly uncomfortable with the situation; however, the girl persists. 'Well?'

'I'd a little fall. And no, I'm not sore,' Connie lies.

'I fell in school before we got our holidays. My cut is all better now.'

'I'm delighted to hear that. We must be careful. And a little bird tells me that you also fell last night,' Connie adds with a hint of mischief.

'No, I didn't!'

'You did—you fell asleep!'

When the giggles peter out, Connie fishes a handful of coins from her bag. 'Get something for yourself and your pal.'

Unlike Abeo, these children have no qualms about accepting her money.

'Look,' Liam says, reappearing and pointing at a man taking a bottle of something fizzy from the fridge. 'He's wearing me!'

Connie recognises her son's face on the back of the customer's sweatshirt. She'd lost count of all the items of clothing that Liam—the real Liam—had bought with his pocket money, featuring his sporting heroes. She knew, one day, her son's face would also grace them.

I knew it.

'Did you do that to her?' Connie looks around; the girl in the pink dress stands before Abeo. This time, her hands rest confrontationally on her tiny hips.

'Sorry?' he politely enquires, attempting to disarm her temerity with his winning smile.

'Her face. My mammy just said to my aunt that you did it.'

Abeo and Connie look towards two adults behind them; they wave frantically at the girl to return.

'Oh, God no,' Connie interjects, approaching them. 'He saved me.'

'Who from?'

'I had a little accident earlier. That's why I said you must be careful, not only in the playground. Especially when you get to my age, you become clumsy.'

'Come on,' Abeo whispers to Connie, leading her outside, 'we should go.'

He places two bags into the motorcycle's top box alongside Connie's handbag. 'I will ask you again: are you sure about this? We can turn around and go back to Kenny's.'

'Yes, go back!' Liam interjects.

'Let's continue, Abeo. Thank you.'

Helmet securely fastened, Connie places her arms tightly around Abeo's waist as they drive west into the night.

CHAPTER TWENTY-FOUR
THEN, SATURDAY NIGHT

'MAM, WHAT ARE you doing out of bed?'

Liam stood at the sink, washing dishes, and gave his mother a look usually reserved for his competitors on the pitch. He'd now exchanged his dapper ensemble for a more comfortable tracksuit. However, his earlier anger remained the same.

'I don't even remember what happened. Did you put me to bed?' Two hours of sleep had helped Connie's form improve, but her head remained cloudy.

'With Mary Elizabeth's help.'

'God.' Now wrapped in her dressing gown, she took a mandarin orange from the fruit bowl and peeled it. She doubted her sensitive stomach would appreciate its acidity, but dehydrated and tired, she needed a sugar rush and something to do with her restless hands. 'Where's everyone?'

'The Steeples.'

'And why didn't you go with them?'

'Oh, I don't know—I didn't fancy coming home to discover my mother unconscious on her bed or face-down in a pool of vomit,' Liam said.

'Connie allowed silence to diffuse the tension. 'Let me help with those dishes.'

'Mam, go back to bed.'

'I doubt I'll do much sleeping now.'

Liam turned away from her; he never remained angry with his mother for long, but he certainly wouldn't give in too quickly tonight.

'Besides,' Connie continued, 'washing up will help me work the alcohol out of my system. Otherwise, I'll be doubled over the toilet all night.'

'Well, if you end up in the bathroom again, be a dear and leave the door unlocked, will you? Even with all my gym training, I couldn't knock it open earlier.'

'Did I lock myself in?'

'You must have had a shower because you were soaking wet.'

She vaguely remembered being submerged in water but had assumed her mind was warning her to hydrate. 'Let me do those dishes.'

Liam threw the J-cloth to her. With her reflexes compromised, it landed plumb on the middle of her head. They both laughed.

'If I ask you a question, Mam, don't lie to me.'

'This sounds ominous.'

'You didn't take anything today, did you?'

'Take?'

'Come on, you know what I'm talking about.'

'Did I make a show of myself?'

'No, you didn't. Nobody saw anything, and Breege did a good job stealing the limelight, but you were out of it. You must be bloody Lazarus because I don't know how you can sit up now and eat your little orange.'

'I'm sorry, I was just anxious.'

'Mam! You promised!'

'I know, I hadn't intended to. I became overwhelmed.'

'And where did you even get the tablets?'

'I swear, there were only a few of them, and I only kept them to … Oh, I don't know. To comfort me, maybe? In the past, it helped me to know they were there just in case.'

'Where is there?'

Connie hesitated. 'In a glass container hidden inside my mattress.'

He raced into the bedroom as Connie dropped onto the kitchen chair. If her son was furious with her, it paled compared to her anger towards herself.

Stupid, stupid woman.

A moment later, Liam returned and handed her the vial. She took it and threw the remaining tablets into the suds.

'And then to drink all that booze,' Liam continued. 'Mixing can be lethal.'

'They're gone now. It's over. I promise. Let's talk about this tomorrow. Or never because it won't happen again. Now, I thought you were going up to The Steeples?'

'I'm not bothering.' Liam wiped the counter next to the sink.

'What? Because of me? I'm fine, and I'll hardly get much sleep tonight, anyway.'

'I'll stay up with you, then.'

'You don't trust me. I can hardly blame you.'

'It's not that.'

'Please. It would make me feel better, especially if I've ruined your day.'

'You haven't ruined my day.'

She could tell that Liam was conflicted.

'After your tea, you're going to bed, right?'

'Exactly, my love.'

He sat beside her. 'I hear you told Mary Elizabeth your secret about talking to me when I'm not around. I hope you know you can talk to me—*for real*—anytime. On the phone or Zoom. Or, better yet, in person. This new phase of my career doesn't mean it's the end of us. You can stay with me in Dublin. The guys you've met adore you, and why wouldn't they?'

'I doubt any of them would be adoring me tonight.'

'Now, now, we already had one party today, let's not have a pity party as well. You did what you did, but we both know it was the last time, right?'

'Right.'

'I hope you liked the presents.'

'I can't believe *you* did what you did. A car! Now, that's definitely something we'll talk about tomorrow, especially seeing as you bought it because—'

'Mam! I trust you. Today was a once-off, you said.'
'It was, I promise.'
'Right, I better head down to that fiancée of mine.'

Connie couldn't remember the final hours of the party; had there been a proposal? Her stomach knotted. She could kick herself for missing one of the most important moments of her son's life.

'Send her my love,' she eventually said, feigning enthusiasm. Mary Elizabeth will fill her in tomorrow morning. 'I'm so happy that you're together. You won't ...?'

'I won't?'

'Abandon her or mistreat her.'

'Mam!'

'I know the answer. It's something someone said earlier.'

'Who?'

'It doesn't matter. You won't, will you?'

'There's only one lady I love more than Jess, and like you, I'll always treat her like royalty. I promise.'

Connie covered the leftovers of Gerry and Jess' cakes with tin foil, and after struggling to rearrange the remaining food and alcohol in the fridge, she placed them on one of the shelves.

'The day hasn't properly sunk in yet. I hope everyone knows how grateful I am.'

'Aside from what happened in the bathroom, it was the best day, Mam. Well, parts of it, at least. And I can't wait to destroy the rest of those cakes tomorrow. Just me and you.'

Walking towards the door, he caught his reflection in the mirror and noticed a red mark staining the back of his coat.

'I bet that was Breege's doing.'

'It's not red wine, is it?'

'I'd say so. She was drinking anything wet towards the end. Our goldfish bowl is probably empty at this stage. I wouldn't like to be her tomorrow.' He cast the jacket aside and gave Connie a peck on the cheek. 'I won't be late, I promise.'

As she filled a glass with water and watched Liam disappear around the side of the cottage, passing her brand-new car, Connie realised she hadn't told him to wear another coat.

He'll catch his death.

* * *

Connie lay diagonally across her bed, tossing and turning. Having initially fallen into a deep sleep, she woke a few hours later battling indigestion, dehydration and, as expected, a headache that resembled two drills piercing through her skull. She overheated when the duvet sat on her restless body and shivered when she tossed it aside. Connie debated what prevented her most from sleeping. The sticky, humid air, the guilt and shame, her early hangover, or the clock-watching she did whenever Liam went out.

He's fine, he's safe.

Kicking the duvet into the corner of the bed again, she reminded herself that Liam had always been the sensible one in his group. She only needed to reflect on how maturely he had treated her earlier that night and throughout her entire battle with addiction. Often, he'd been the parent in the relationship. Connie trusted him. He'd be fine.

Where is he?

Yes, he often stayed with friends or, more recently, with Jess, but without fail, Connie would get a message with updates on his whereabouts. But tonight, she hadn't received a single text from him. So many horrific things had happened in the village over the years, and danger was never more in the air than when people were under the influence. If anyone could vouch for that, Connie could. Worse again, the river had claimed the lives of two men in the recent past, both drunk when they'd fallen in. The new railings helped, but they didn't make anyone invincible.

What if Liam is in the river, struggling to stay afloat? Or dying from hypothermia? What if he misses training on Monday? Will he be kicked off the team?

'Connie! Go to sleep!'

She turned over the pillow and told herself to stop being so ridiculous. The long-running joke was that she hadn't enjoyed a good night's sleep since first becoming a mother, and that was close to the truth. Every night, questions raced through her mind. Did he have enough to eat? Did he enjoy his day at school? Is he losing out because he doesn't have a father figure? It would take her ages to fall asleep, and when she eventually did, it would rarely be for long.

Conceding that any additional sleep would elude her, Connie decided to make some tea, a new herbal variety they'd recently started stocking in the newsagent's. It was a fusion of lavender and chamomile, but whether it would prove helpful remained to be seen. She filled the kettle. Even though the celebrations had ended on a sour note, she hoped everyone had a good time and Breege's destructive ways wouldn't be everyone's lasting memory. Her main fear was that their indiscretions, especially her own, would appear on social media.

Did I throw someone's phone into the bush?

So many guests, expected and unexpected. So many presents lined up against the wall. She wouldn't need to buy a moisturiser or bottle of perfume for another forty years. Leaning against the counter, she placed her hand on Teddy's grandmother's necklace, hidden under her singlet, and made a mental note to call him in the morning to thank him for his kindness and, of course, to arrange that tea date she'd promised.

She now wondered what came of Bosco and his stars. Ending up on the bathroom floor hardly made her a desirable candidate for a second date. She laughed, remembering some of his delightfully corny chat-up lines. Was there even a kiss at some stage? But her smile immediately vanished after realising the gift she'd bought Liam—the bottle of Moët in the wooden champagne box—was missing.

It was on the table before I went to bed. I placed it there to give it to Liam in the morning.

Connie scanned the kitchen, accepting that she could easily have moved it without remembering. Reaching the table, she realised one of the untouched boxes of beer had also vanished. She opened the fridge. There were at least four bottles of wine there when Connie went to bed; now, they were gone, too. That was when she spotted, or didn't spot, something that made her body stiffen.

The car.

Earlier in the evening, Liam had parked it at the side of the house, out of sight from curious neighbours. The kitchen window should have given her the perfect view. But Connie realised that Liam must have come home at some stage, raided the house for alcohol and driven off somewhere, probably to an afterparty.

How did I not hear them? And why did he drive? How could he be so stupid?

Connie stormed into her bedroom, grabbed her phone, and dialled her son's number. No answer. She called for a second, third and fourth time. Still no answer. Peering through the window, she hoped the car had just been moved to the front of the cottage. Maybe Liam had wanted to show off in front of his pals, but it was nowhere to be seen. She tried reaching Jess and then Mary Elizabeth, but the outcome was the same: no answer. The kettle came to a boil in the kitchen. Tea, no matter how much lavender or chamomile was in it, would be of any use to her now. Connie was too flustered to cry, too anxious to scream. What she wouldn't give for another couple of tablets. Unfortunately, they had been unceremoniously dumped down the drain. As she was about to inspect the garden to see if the car was parked elsewhere, her phone vibrated. It was Liam.

'Oh my God, Liam, where are you? Please don't tell me you've been driving.'

'Mam,' he interrupted, the word dropping like a bomb in Connie's ear. 'I'm in trouble.'

CHAPTER TWENTY-FIVE
NOW

AS ABEO NAVIGATES the narrow, winding track leading to the caravan park, Connie holds him tightly to prevent herself from falling into the gorse bushes lining the route. In her youth, Connie had spent a portion of a rain-soaked summer with her parents in a similar caravan park outside Galway, cut short when her mother fell victim to septicaemia following an unpleasant encounter with a rusty nail. Or, at least, that was the story the girl had been told while being dragged away from her new friends on the beach.

Abeo dismounts the motorcycle and hoists the wide gate against the ditch, securing it in the overgrowth. Connie admires his strength, not for the first time today. His feet are firmly rooted into the ground, and his every move, even the simple opening of a gate, has power and intent— the antithesis of her current, hesitant form. Connie feels connected to this kind and protective man in a way she has never experienced.

'This place is run down, but you know that,' Abeo says as they walk the remaining part of the journey. 'If you change your mind, let me know, and we can come up with another plan.'

Connie always smiles at the memory of seven-year-old Liam rushing home from school, having discovered that oil and water will never mix no matter 'how much you swish and swirl'. Today, if she is oil, everybody in her orbit is water, and she needs to be alone.

'I can already tell it will be perfect.'

'The park mightn't be in good condition, but the views out onto the ocean are spectacular. You'll have to wait until morning to see them properly, but you can hear the waves if you listen. Can you?'

'I can, I certainly can.'

The fresh, salty air awakens her. It truly feels like the edge of the world here. Whatever direction she looks, there are caravans, lines of them. They pass a crazy golf course overrun with moss and weeds, and there's a tennis court in the distance. The collapsed net suggests it has been a while since anyone has enjoyed a rally there.

'You always liked tennis, didn't you?' she whispers to an unimpressed Liam, now trailing them. 'Was there any sport you didn't excel in?'

'Shhh, listen to your man. Otherwise, you might miss learning about the park's evening entertainment and restaurant opening hours.' Liam's voice brims with derision. 'I wonder if there's an on-site masseuse because I've got a terrible knot in my neck after that journey here.'

'There aren't too many shops nearby,' Abeo informs Connie, guiding her around a mess of shattered glass, 'although the bus goes in and out of town every few hours. That could have changed since we were all last here, but we can double-check. There might even be bicycles somewhere. You'll probably need clothes, or did you leave a suitcase somewhere? I could collect it for you.'

'I'll manage,' she assures him. The sparseness of her wardrobe is the least of her concerns. 'Did you come here on holiday?'

'One of the guys on the site had a stag party.'

'Yes, of course, you mentioned that.'

'They've been coming here for the last few years. Simon inherited it from an uncle. To be honest, the novelty is gone. When you have a hangover, the journey home is too long and bumpy, so I don't think anybody will bother you except a few stray dogs. I was only here once. I'd only started at the site after …'

'Dad died?'

Abeo nods as he stops outside a caravan, the final one before the water's edge.

'This is yours,' he announces, resting the motorcycle in front of it before taking the shopping bags and a flashlight from the trunk. Unlike its counterparts, Connie's caravan has no broken windows or flat tyres. She holds the torch while he connects the battery and tinkers with a gas bottle.

'There, at least we can boil a kettle now.' He pulls a step from under the caravan. 'It's slippy, be careful.' With a hefty tug, he opens the door and flips a switch; the lights flicker on.

The caravan's size is modest and could benefit from dusting and cleaning, but other than that, Connie feels it suits her needs. There is even bottled water by the kitchenette. In the bedroom, blinds hang by a thread while peeling peach wallpaper reveals white styrofoam insulation underneath, making her wonder how long these caravans have been on site. Clean sheets and towels are wrapped in plastic on the bedside locker.

'Do you think I might be allowed to stay longer than a few weeks?' she asks Liam, sitting on the lumpy mattress.

'I don't know, Mam, judging by what we saw coming through the park, this looks to be a destination in high demand!'

'Do you think?'

'I'm kidding. But I'm not kidding about you calling me. Please, Mam. You've no idea what thoughts are going through my mind in Portugal, wondering where you've been since your release. Although,' he continues, looking around, 'the reality is far worse.'

'I'll call you in the morning.'

He kisses her cheek. 'We get up at four-thirty for training. I'll be waiting.'

Connie returns outside, where Abeo places a plate of food on a table. 'I could open a restaurant here at this rate,' she teases. 'Connie's Camping Cuisine has a nice ring to it.'

'Your dad mentioned you always liked to joke.'

'Did he?'

Abeo nods. 'He spoke about you a lot, although he called you by another name. What was it?'

'Imelda.'

'That's exactly it. And he kept mentioning a two-legged mouse for some reason. Does that make sense to you?'

'It certainly does.'

She sits beside Abeo on a bench, the moon silvering the vast ocean in front of them. The rolling waves soothe the two visitors as they sit in companionable silence and eat crackers, cheese and ham. There are several questions Connie would like to ask Abeo about his life, but it has never been in her nature to pry, unlike that curious child in the petrol station. Whatever retribution he needs to pay for stealing from her father is complete. She suspects he, too, would prefer to keep the conversation surface-level.

'Do you like boating or fishing?' she asks.

'I like hiking. Are you a walker?'

Her mind immediately races back thirty-odd years to the day a Brownie leader on a recruitment drive called to their door.

'We've lots of fun activities,' the woman promised Connie. 'Next week, we're hiking in the Cooley Mountains.'

'The only place this one walks to is the fridge,' her mother scoffed before slamming the door shut.

'Maybe hiking is something I could start doing,' Connie tells Abeo.

'There's a hike you'll like. It brings you to a cave where pirates hid treasure. And they say there's gold stashed in there to this day.'

'That's one way of paying my rent, I suppose.'

'Do you need money?'

'No, I was trying to make a joke, but I've obviously lost my touch.'

'You would tell me if you did.'

'I wouldn't, but thank you. I'll never forget your kindness.'

Connie tilts her head back. The constant Northern Star has already appeared, and she wonders if 'Connie Major' will shine tonight.

'This should keep me going until I get back to Kenny's house,' Abeo says.

'You're leaving tonight?'

'Steady on, Mam!' Liam says, hunching down between them.

'I could stay if you wanted,' Abeo replies evenly, 'and then leave early in the morning?'

'It's completely up to you.'

'I'll sleep on the couch then if that's okay.'

'Whatever suits you best.'

They sit in silence again. 'Would you like more cheese?' Connie finally says.

'If I did, I'd have to spend the entire weekend in the gym.'

'You look after yourself, I can tell.'

'Mam! Look at you and your flirting! Who knew!'

'I'm not flirting! Does it sound like I am? I don't mean to—I promise I don't.'

'I go to the gym, although nowhere near as often as I'd like to. This job in the village is demanding. I have to get buses up and down from Kells. My car broke down last month and it will be expensive to repair.'

Connie makes a mental note to slip money into his jacket before going to bed. Aside from the petrol and groceries, Abeo also paid for a tyre. Did he also lose out on a day's wage bringing her here?

'You like what you do? Your work on the site?' she asks.

'I haven't much choice because I have two teenage daughters.'

'How old are they?'

'Nineteen and seventeen. One has just started college, and the other is about to. "Brains to burn"—that's what everyone says about them, and they'd be right.'

'Go on,' Liam prods, 'ask if he's still with their mother.'

'I'll do no such thing! It's none of my business!'

'It can be difficult sometimes because their mother isn't around,' Abeo continues, almost overhearing the imaginary conversation. 'We split up a few years ago.'

'Oh, I'm sorry to hear that.'

Abeo gives a resigned, I-tried-everything-I-could shrug. 'We haven't seen her in a few months. She texted our eldest to say she was in Liverpool—probably a good move. Sorry, you don't want to hear my problems.'

'I do. I mean, only if you want to discuss them, of course.'

'Long story short, she spent money we didn't have and borrowed from the wrong people. It's actually why I … It doesn't matter.'

'Stole from Granddad,' Liam interjects.

'What about you?' Abeo continues. 'Do you still have a good relationship with your son?'

'After everything that happened that night? It has certainly changed,' Connie says, considering her words. 'He was my only visitor in prison and came often. But I hope, one day, we'll properly reconnect in a happier environment.'

'It must have been a tough two years for him. I've no idea how he has remained so focused on rugby.'

'Well, he struggles. How could he not?'

Liam releases a sigh. 'Can I get an "amen"?'

'He's such an amazing sportsman,' Abeo continues. 'My daughters are big fans.'

'I'm happy to hear he inspires others. He definitely is an inspiration to me.'

'I know he has talked about forgiveness, which has impressed me. He has said he loves you as much now as before the crash. That shows how close your bond is.'

'It's true,' Liam tells her. 'Nothing will ever break us. But you already know that.'

'Could you join him wherever in the world he is?'

Connie shakes her head. 'No, I won't be joining him anywhere for now.'

'And why not, Mam?' Liam stands in front of her. 'You know you can join me anytime you want. I've told you time and time again.'

'It's your big moment now, Liam. Your first World Cup. This is what you've spent your entire life working towards. You need to do this alone.'

'You mean *you* need to do this alone,' Liam corrects as he disappears.

After a moment, Abeo clears the leftovers, and they both return to the caravan.

'It's been a long day,' he says. 'I'll be gone before you wake.'

'Are you sure you won't take my bed, and I'll sleep on the couch?'

'You'll do no such thing. And if you need anything after I'm gone, call me. I'll leave my number.'

'You've been … Thank you.'

'I can come back.'

'Don't dream of it. You have work and your girls.'

'I'd like to. So long as you'd like me to.'

'I would,' Connie replies, and she means it. 'Just not yet, though.'

They share a final smile.

'Goodnight, Connie Maguire. I look forward to seeing you again.'

CHAPTER TWENTY-SIX
THEN, SUNDAY MORNING

EVEN THOUGH SHE'D lived in the village her entire life, everything around Connie seemed unfamiliar that morning—Gerry's café, the pharmacy, St Gerard Majella's Church. She had never noticed the iron grate underneath the newsagent's window before. And what about the splash of green paint across the side of the post office—how long had it been there? The crooked lamppost, the lopsided bin. She could have been passing through an entirely different village. Everyone's pride and joy, the double-lotus fountain, looked like a toy.

Did I visit it earlier tonight?

While the streetlights illuminated her way for now, she gripped a torch in one hand and called Liam repeatedly with the other. Still no answer. After revealing that he was in trouble five minutes earlier, he hung up; the light ping that signalled the end of the call never sounded so devastating to Connie. All her senses were now heightened: the light breeze, usually so welcome on a muggy autumnal night, slapped her across her face. The odour of leftover chips, doused in salt and vinegar, made her nauseous. The hood of her yellow raincoat clung to her moist neck.

Where is he?

The only sounds were her footfall and pounding heart. The red-bricked, three-storey Steeples pub revealed itself in the distance. Whatever late-night tomfoolery that Cyril, the owner, had promised now appeared to have ended. The blinds were down, the lights off. Bin bags bulged with the night's indulgences. Something was amiss. The front door appeared stronger and sturdier than before, intimidating even. She banged on it for several moments and waited. Nothing.

'Cyril!' she shouted. 'Are you there?'

Connie climbed on a nearby bench usually occupied by gossiping smokers and banged on the window. Again, nothing. Rounding the building, she rang the doorbell to Cyril's apartment.

'Jesus Christ, it's five o'clock in the morning!' he groaned, opening a window. 'If you're looking for the party, it's in Kavanagh's barn.'

He emphasised his displeasure by walloping the window shut. Connie rushed across the stone bridge towards the barn. The lion mascot standing tall outside the petrol station looked sinister, somehow. She reasoned that Kavanagh's farm could be reached in about five minutes if she maintained her pace. A flurry of questions stormed her mind.

What has happened in the barn? Did a fight break out? Was somebody hurt? Why isn't Liam answering his phone?

The derelict barn had been empty for as long as anyone could remember. It witnessed teenagers smoking their first cigarettes, enjoying their first drink and sharing their first kiss. The joke in the village was, 'if walls could talk', and even though said walls were crumbling by the day, it didn't prevent locals from visiting and throwing the occasional party there.

With the help of her torch and, at times, the moon, playing hide-and-seek with a lone cloud, Connie navigated the country road without falling. She knew the route well, although, for many years, had avoided it as it was near Nick's family home. There were days when her younger self didn't have the energy to field his parents' complaints at not being given more access to Liam or listen to their disgust that the boy hadn't received their family name.

'It's tradition!' they would scream at her almost every time they met in those frosty months following the birth.

How Connie wished she had the tenacity to remind them of their son's disregard for 'tradition' by fleeing the village, leaving her a single mother who had not yet been old enough to vote. She now spotted the roof of their red-bricked house peeping out above a long line of fir trees. The main property belonged to Nick's brother, Barry, after their parents downsized to the bungalow at the bottom of the garden. Drawing closer, she noticed several lights within.

Is Nick involved in all this somehow?

She debated whether to call in or continue to the barn: maybe Nick and Barry were simply awake, having a late drink or playing poker. Her instinct told her to continue towards the barn. However, after clearing their house, Connie heard her name called: it was Barry. He leaned against a fence, and despite the darkness, she could sense his distress.

'What's happened? Where's Liam?'

'I don't know.' Barry's voice was noticeably missing its usual verve. She realised he was drenched in blood.

'What happened, Barry? Whose blood is that?'

'He just …' a dazed Barry began but then drifted off into a trance. 'He has never changed. He never will.'

'Nick? What did he do, Barry?'

'He lost the bloody plot. I've never seen anything like it before.'

'What happened? Tell me!'

'Don't shout at me, Connie!' he snapped, rubbing his balding head to calm himself; she'd never seen this usually jocular man so wretched, so tragic. 'We had a few drinks. I should have known better. He was furious that you had a go at him. He said you were insulting. Then he disappeared to get chips.'

Connie could barely process what she was hearing. She had accepted that Nick had manipulated their earlier, brief exchange to curry favour with their son—it was straight out of his playbook—but he had actually convinced himself that he had been the victim, that she had mistreated him somehow. But his interpretation was patently false. Connie knew his ego was legendary, but only now was she fully realising how detached Nick was from reality and that unless you pandered to his every whim, the narcissist would unravel. Her anger and anxiety bubbled to the surface. Her vision distorted; she could barely make out Barry's face despite him standing in front of her.

'When he came back, he was grand. He said he pushed you into the fountain. Did he?'

Did he? Was that why I had that flashback in the square? Was that why I was all wet?

'He was probably lying,' Barry continued. 'We had another beer. His girlfriend was with us, but then we all fell asleep.'

'And then what?'

'Then he woke up and started smashing things for no reason. The whole house is a bombshell. His girlfriend—what's her name?'

'I don't know!'

'She fled, probably got a taxi in the village. There's usually one outside The Steeples on Saturday.'

Connie accepted that Nick had been the catalyst for Liam's call. 'Where is Nick now?'

'After he calmed down, he got a message saying there was a lock-in over at The Steeples. Before I knew it, he'd gone.'

'But there's no one in The Steeples now. I've just been there. Cyril said they'd all gone to the barn.'

'That explains it.'

'*Explains what, Barry?*'

'Nick came back about an hour and a half ago, taking drink from the cabinet. I tried to stop him, but he punched me.' Barry gestured towards the blood all over his clothes. 'Then he disappeared again.'

'Did you see Liam with him?'

Barry nodded.

'Were they driving?'

'I didn't see a car. I didn't hear one.'

'But you saw Liam?'

'Definitely, he waved at me. He didn't realise I was dripping in blood. They stood about twenty metres from where you're now standing. They'd boxes of beer, wine—the lot. Champagne even. There were about fifty of them, possibly more. Someone had flashing lights—the things you'd see at a disco. Or am I making that up? I'm confused. What I do remember is how happy Liam looked at being out with his dad. He even put his arm around him as they walked off.'

Walked off? But why did Liam then come home again and take the car? Or has it been stolen?

Earlier, she could never imagine wishing her shiny present would be robbed. Now, she desperately hoped that that was the case.

'This doesn't make sense. What time was this at, Barry?'

'About an hour and a half ago, I told you!'

'And what have you been doing since then, you bastard? Why didn't you follow them? Or call Teddy at the station? Or call me?' Connie had never experienced this level of anger before. 'Did you think that everything would resolve itself on its own? That Nick's mood would magically improve with a few more drinks and a dance around the barn? Look what he did to you for crying out loud! Liam has just called me—he's in trouble, Barry. In trouble!'

'What kind of trouble?'

She didn't even wait to give a response.

* * *

To reach Kavanagh's barn, Connie had to pass a narrow lane overgrown with bushes and dead snags. Faint sounds fluttered in the distance—conversations vying to be heard over the beats of techno music. The painful throbbing noise offered Connie a strange comfort: if the party were in full swing, perhaps the crisis from earlier had resolved itself. She pictured Nick sleeping in a pool of vomit before being greeted by the hangover from hell.

No more than he deserves.

She called Liam's phone for what she imagined was the hundredth time, conceding that, like before, it would go unanswered. She stopped abruptly. By a tree, a red vixen stood in front of her sleeping cub, the growing morning sunshine glistened on their coats. When Connie inched closer to them, the vixen's amber eyes enlarged and sharpened, weighing up this possible threat of danger. There weren't many aspects of her old school days that Connie remembered well, but enshrined in her mind was the little-known fact that, after birth, fox cubs couldn't see, hear or walk. It was left to their mother to care for them. Support them. Guide them. Protect them.

Connie redialled her son's number and, after a moment, heard ringing nearby. The melody, a sped-up version of 'Ireland's Call', was instantly recognisable.

'Liam! Can you hear me?'

She scrambled around the tree, ensuring not to disturb the vixen and her cub. The field, veiled in a light fog, left little doubt about how neglected the farm had been in recent years. Blades of grass soared a metre high. Rusted tractors lay strewn across the land with abandon. Bashing the weeds and reeds that crossed her path, she struggled with her footing but knew her son was close.

'Liam!'

Connie detected the whine of a car engine. The deeper she ventured into the field, the louder the sound became. She ran but tripped, dropping her torch and phone. A rock ripped a gash across her forehead. Blood streamed out, dripping all over her face and yellow raincoat. Returning to her feet, she staggered further into the field and noticed a pool of light skimming the surface of the overgrowth: the car's headlights.

CHAPTER TWENTY-SEVEN

NOW

CONNIE SITS BOLT upright; her skin and bedsheets are soaked. Outside, an engine starts. She looks out the window and sees Abeo and the motorcycle disappear past the gates.

A clock hangs on the wall in the kitchenette. Instead of two o'clock, as it indicates, Connie imagines it's closer to six.

'You could do with a coffee, Mother dearest,' Liam says, leaning against the counter. 'I think your friend reckoned on that.' He points towards the table where Abeo has laid out the shopping. 'It looks like he's bought you enough for a month! And he's even left out a first aid kit. I know you don't need me telling you this, but you must keep Breege's handiwork clean to avoid infection.'

'I don't think I'll ever be able to repay Abeo for his kindness, his generosity,' she says. Alongside his purchases is a note with information about buses and walking trails.

At the bottom, he has scribbled his phone number, 'in case you need it'.

'I know what will immediately improve this place,' Liam says, pointing to her handbag on the seat.

Connie retrieves the framed photograph of herself and her son. Even though it had been subjected to a beating from Breege and a cross-country motorcycle ride, miraculously, the glass remains unbroken. She caresses her son's young, muddied face. Without fail, following each match, he would run to her as she waited on the sidelines. Together, they would cry tears of joy or tears of pain. Connie gives the photograph pride of place in the middle of the table.

'What more do I need?'

'Well, I'll tell you what you *need* to do. You need to call me. Now.'

'What am I going to say to you? I know you mean well, wanting to help, but I—'

'Need to do it alone. I can get on board with that, Mam. Well, not really, but I can't get on board with silence. So, *please*, call me.'

Connie removes her phone from the bag and dials her son as she did dozens of times on the night of the crash.

'Hello, my love,' she says when he finally answers. 'Can you hear me? I don't think the signal is great. There you are. Look, don't give out to me. I'm sorry I haven't been in touch, but I want you to know I'm fine. And safe. I am, really.'

Connie listens as Liam berates her for turning her phone off—'I've been going out of my mind with worry'—then attempts to persuade her to join him in Portugal and allow him to take care of her and protect her.

'I need you here with me,' he tells her, his once-confident voice having long deserted him.

'I know. That's why I didn't want to answer your calls. I didn't want you to persuade me to fly over to Portugal. I will, eventually. Just not today.'

'But why, Mam? I'm shattered, broken, absolutely destroyed. I miss Jess every single minute. I miss *you* every single minute.'

'Focus on your training and forget about me.'

'I'm not going to forget about you.'

'For now. Just for now. Be patient. I'll be in touch soon. I love you.'

'I love you, too. More than you'll ever know.'

CHAPTER TWENTY-EIGHT
THEN, SUNDAY MORNING

CONNIE TRIED TO make sense of the scene. The Mini Cooper was soldered into a tree. Nick's lifeless body was draped over the glove compartment, his face propped against the smashed windowpane. Jess sat slumped between the driver and passenger seats. Connie's legs gave way underneath her, and she collapsed to the ground.

'Where's Liam? Liam?'

Connie crawled into the car. How she hoped it was all some fever dream. She pushed Nick out onto the field before checking the pulse of her son's beautiful fiancée, even though she knew the outcome. She placed her raincoat over the ravaged body, shroud-like, as if it would safeguard her somehow. Before she knew it, Connie had doubled over and was vomiting uncontrollably.

Where's Liam? Where is he?

She realised the phone's ringing had ended and, in its place, heard a whisper of tears. This mother immediately recognised them, having listened to them many times before. When Sally Furlong ended their short relationship in senior infants. When Fionn Murphy mocked him for only having one parent in sixth class. When he missed a conversion kick in the final of the Under-16s World Cup. These tears belonged to her son. He sat behind a second tree, his face stunned.

But he's alive, Connie repeated as she reached him, examining his face to ensure he wasn't injured or concussed. There wasn't a scratch on him; he must have been wearing his seatbelt.

'I just called for help,' he mumbled. 'The police will be here in a few minutes. But it's no use. I've killed them. *I killed them.*'

'It was an accident—'

Before Connie could finish her sentence, the unmistakable smell of alcohol enveloped her. The reality of what had just happened began to sink in: her son, probably twenty times over the limit, had driven a car and killed his father and the young woman he planned to marry.

'He was out of control,' Liam began explaining. 'We were at the barn. The music was playing. Everyone was dancing. I looked around for him. For Dad. I couldn't find him in the crowd. Then I realised he'd come back outside. His body was shaking. A seizure, an epileptic seizure. Brought on by the drink. And the flashing lights.'

'Go on.'

'Jess rang for an ambulance. They said they'd be over two hours. Two hours! There was a big fire in one of the warehouses outside Drogheda. They were busy, they said. "Get someone to bring him in," they said. I had no choice, Mam. I had to run home and get the car. Your car. Your birthday present. Drive him to the hospital.'

If it weren't for the fact that he'd already died, she would have killed Nick there and then with her bare hands.

'Jess stayed by his side until I drove back,' Liam continued, reliving the details beat by beat. 'She can't drive—God, why can't she drive?—and wouldn't let me go to the hospital alone. I was telling them to put on their seatbelts. He couldn't, of course. Jess tried to help him—helping others, always helping others. Then, out of nowhere, he punched her!'

'What?'

'Out of nowhere. The seizure seemed to end, but things got worse. I'd never seen anything so vicious in my life. He hit her, then hit me as I was driving. On my ear. I couldn't see where I was going. Then, I killed them. Oh my God, I killed all three of them!'

'Three? Is there someone else?' Just as Connie was about to race to the car, Liam stopped her.

'Jess was pregnant. Four months. That's why I wanted to get engaged. But what does that bloody matter now? I killed my entire family!'

'I'm still here, my love, and I'm not going anywhere. And it wasn't your fault. You had no choice.'

'Mam! I've had about twenty drinks. What was I thinking? I thought he would die from the seizure. If I hadn't drunk so much, I'd have been able to … Oh, I don't know!'

Connie didn't need him to reveal the amount he'd consumed. Between the slurring and the smell, he was utterly drunk, and a simple breathalyser would verify that. A police siren cut through the brief silence.

'Mam, Mam! What am I going to do?' He grabbed her by the arms, coming to his knees.

'It's not your fault,' Connie repeated as if that would make it true. But it was his fault, she knew. Of course, it would be considered an emergency, and his father had attacked him, but there was no getting away from the fact that he drove a car while heavily under the influence, killing two people.

Three.

Her son's life was ruined. Connie was no legal expert, but she doubted he would avoid jail time even if they managed to hire the best lawyer. Granted, it wouldn't be a life sentence, but even a few months would end his glittering rugby career. He would be an outcast in the village and throughout the entire country.

The siren grew louder, deafening them both.

'We'll get through this together. I won't leave you.'

'Jess is gone. Our baby. Because of me.'

When Liam turned towards the oncoming police car, Connie saw the gravity of the situation dawning on him.

'I'm going to prison, Mam. What does it matter? Sure, what else do I have to live for now?'

The image of the vixen and her cub raced through Connie's mind. She needed to protect her son but didn't know how. Whatever happened to Liam, Connie would be there, holding his hand, supporting him, loving him. Her God-fearing mother had never protected Connie, never shielded her from the world's many challenges, and when they did emerge, the woman refused to become her daughter's ally. Connie had made a vow early in life never to replicate this fractured relationship. She would always be there for Liam, no matter what. She wouldn't turn her back on her child in his hour of need. Like that red vixen, she would defend her cub to the bitter end, no matter what. It was her maternal instinct. Her vulpine instinct.

'Liam, listen to me,' she said, her voice suddenly full of authority. 'You must do as I say, like you've always done. You will join the national squad as arranged. You will train every single hour that God sends. You will help Ireland qualify for the World Cup, okay? And you will score and win and lift the Webb Ellis Cup.'

'But—'

'Children will have posters of you on their bedroom doors and walls. They will wear t-shirts with your face on them. You will fulfil your destiny.'

'How can that happen? I'm going to prison!'

Connie scanned the field. 'Nobody saw you drive the car, did they?'

'I don't think so. What does that matter?'

'It matters because we will tell the guards I was driving.'

Liam's earlier vulnerability quickly made way for outrage. 'What? Are you crazy? No way, no way, no way!'

Connie placed her hand firmly over his mouth. 'I'm not asking you. I'm telling you, Liam.'

'But you've been drinking, too! You've been drinking all day, Mam! And eating tablets. You even locked yourself in the bathroom earlier!'

'It doesn't matter.'

'Of course, it matters! I'm not having my mother go to prison for something she didn't do. Are you mad?'

'Hello?' came a voice in the distance. 'Can anyone hear me?'

'Please, Liam. Do as I say.'

'How much did you drink, Mam?' he whispered urgently. 'Tell me.'

The tragedy of the past thirty minutes had certainly sharpened her mind, and she had just vomited, but adrenaline would not negate her day's consumption entirely. She had about eight glasses of cava, a few glasses of sangria, and a couple of other drinks that people had handed her. And, of course, the tablets, the many tablets. She remained well over the limit, that much was certain.

'Over here, Jack. I can see the headlights.'

'And I called the police,' Liam continued, 'they know I am here.'

'Did you tell them that you were driving?'

'No, but—'

'And my fingerprints are all over the car. I've just been in it! And they are also there from earlier. When you first gave it to me as a present. A beautiful, thoughtful present. And look,' she added, pointing towards the gash on her forehead when she'd tripped crossing the field, 'I'm already covered in blood.'

'But Mam—'

'We'll say I followed you on foot and took the keys from you, and I wouldn't let you drive. I wouldn't let you get into the car after you'd first driven it here from our house. This plan will work. *It has to work.*'

The improvised plan was flawed, and she was sure other inaccuracies would emerge—would Barry contradict her, for instance—but surely the courts would ignore them, considering she was taking responsibility and pleading guilty.

Two gardaí appeared in front of them. One of them was, of course, Teddy. His colleague, someone Connie didn't recognise, called for an ambulance and additional backup.

'Concepta? Liam? Are you all right?' Teddy enquired, his habitually emotionless face finally abandoning him. 'What on earth happened? Please, don't tell me either of you were driving. It smells like a brewery here!'

He scrutinised them and, with great reluctance, asked: 'Which of you was driving?'

The mother and son shared a look: while shattered, their bond remained impenetrable.

'Liam was, but we need your help, Teddy,' Connie explained in a hush.

It instantly dawned on this by-the-book officer what the only woman he had ever loved was on the verge of asking. Pre-empting the request, he shook his head.

'No, Concepta, I won't.'

'You have to, Teddy,' she pleaded.

'No.' In all his life, this rule-following man had never so much as swatted a fly, let alone facilitated duplicity as grave as this.

'I'm begging you.'

'You're manipulating me, Concepta.'

'All he was doing was helping his father.'

'Nick? What has he got to do with this? Was he in the car?'

Connie looked over Teddy's shoulder towards his younger colleague, who was making a phone call; time was not her ally.

'His body was convulsing. It was probably an epileptic seizure—he has a history of them. And then he attacked Jess while Liam was driving him to the hospital.'

'I've never seen so much anger,' Liam stuttered.

'Why didn't you run to one of the neighbouring houses and ask for a lift?'

'Because I wasn't thinking straight!'

'Connie,' Teddy said, putting together the bones of a plan, 'from my experience, a judge will be sympathetic to a son trying to help a parent.'

'The ambulance was never going to arrive on time,' Liam said, his mind focusing for the first time since the crash, 'two hours, they told me on the phone. I had no choice.'

'Exactly,' Teddy continued, encouraged. 'We can hire the best lawyer.'

'Money is no object,' Liam added.

'And, if we're lucky, the sentence will be relatively light. Six months, maybe a year.'

'A year?' The temporary jolt of hope Liam had just experienced abandoned him altogether.

'No, Teddy!' Connie cut in. 'This will destroy Liam's career. He's supposed to start training on Monday.'

Their discussion was interrupted when the second guard returned. 'Jesus Christ, who was driving?'

Teddy lowered himself to Connie's level. 'Concepta, you're not thinking straight. Do you want to know what charges you'll face? Dangerous driving occasioning death. Two deaths. Driving under the influence of alcohol occasioning death. Two deaths.' He looked over towards the car. 'Is that your birthday present that everyone in the country has been talking about all night? Is it registered? Insured? If not, you can add those to the list of charges. You're not talking about a slap on the wrist—it could be five years, even more.'

'Oh God,' Liam cried.

'I can't let him go to jail, Teddy. His life will be destroyed.'

'And if you take the fall, do you think yours won't?'

'He's right, Mam. It's my fault, and I need to take responsibility.'

'My life is destroyed either way! Don't you both see that? Do you think I'll return to my normal life after this? My life has also ended tonight, but Liam's doesn't have to. Teddy,' she said firmly. 'You must help us. *Please.*'

'If you plead guilty, you realise what's ahead of you? A guaranteed jail sentence. Shunned by the community and by the country, given Liam's profile. Frontpage coverage. Are you willing to make that sacrifice? I don't think you fully understand what you're suggesting.'

'But that's exactly it, Teddy, I do understand. I really do.'

'If I help, and I'm not saying I will, but if I do, I can never, ever speak to you again. *Ever.*'

Connie nodded her head.

'Who was driving?' the guard repeated. Given the devastation behind him, there wasn't a hint of compassion in his voice.

Connie removed the blue sapphire necklace and returned it to Teddy. The three shared one final look. Defeated, Teddy took his grandmother's necklace from Connie and slowly rose to his feet.

'She was.'

'Who's "she"?'

'Concepta. Connie Maguire.'

CHAPTER TWENTY-NINE
NOW, MORNING

'SOME FRESH AIR, clear the cobwebs?' Liam suggests, standing by the caravan door.

'You read my mind.'

Connie removes the pills and tablets from the first aid kit. She holds them in one hand and opens the door with the other. In addition to her own, about twelve caravans are visible to her. She wanders along the cracked and overgrown pathway and explores her new home. Despite its neglected state, the toys and sporting equipment scattered across the ground suggest this park once welcomed many families, providing a backdrop for a profusion of memories. It comforts Connie.

Liam, trailing behind her, is even more unimpressed by the ghostly park than the night before.

'Don't mind all those pills in your hand, Mam—you'll have to stock up on tetanus injections. Look at all the rusty nails and broken glass on the ground. Why do you think Abeo was so reluctant for you to come here? You're literally at the edge of the world, completely alone.'

The downside of being the mother of someone famous means she must forgo her anonymity, so disappearing off everyone's radar, at least until the morbid intrigue has petered out, is the best solution. For now, she needs neither the cruelty of foes nor the kindness of friends.

But when the warmth of the sunrise suddenly envelopes her, Connie is reminded that she is not, in fact, alone. Here, in the middle of nature, she is amongst allies. Here, there is no judgement, no recrimination, no hatred. Here, she will be free from name-calling and assaults. Here, she will be protected. Nature accepts Connie for who she is and won't demand answers, which she still can't give … and may never be able to provide.

'She's looking after you now,' the tarot reader said the evening before. Connie now knows exactly who he was referencing.

Mother Nature.

In front of the tennis court, Connie notices steps leading to the shore and sits on the top tier, ignoring the many midges dancing around her. The damp, cold stone against her body, coupled with the sea air, eliminates her grogginess.

Liam joins her. 'Not a bad view, in fairness.'

They look out at the ocean, where a handful of fishing trawlers provide company to the gulls soaring overhead. Connie can make out land in the distance; she hasn't gotten her bearings yet but supposes it must be one of the islands along Ireland's west coast.

'Will you be lonely here, Mammy Maguire?'

'Not with you beside me, getting up to mischief.'

They remain silent for several moments, absorbing their new home.

'I can't believe I let you—'

'You didn't let me do anything, Liam. We've been through this a hundred times since. It was my choice. It was completely my choice.'

'But you don't deserve this. The crash was my fault, not yours. Haven't you been through enough over the past twenty-one months? You must stop punishing yourself for something you didn't even do.'

'It doesn't work that way.'

'Explain to me how it works then!' he snaps, his unpredictable temper getting the better of him. 'Over the past twenty-four hours, you've made every effort to self-sabotage. To deny yourself any sliver of happiness. And I'm not talking about bloody champagne and caviar—I'm talking about the most basic pleasures. No food, no home, no friends. First, you stayed in that kippy guesthouse in Dublin, even though I've been lodging thousands into your account. And now, you're living where there's barely any running water. I know I promised to drop the subject, but why can't you come to Portugal, like I said to you on the phone just now, and let me take care of you? The way you've always taken care of me.'

'It doesn't work that way.'

'Then explain to me how it works!'

'Liam, stop, please! That night, I didn't just take the legal responsibility away from you, but I also removed the emotional burden. Jess died, along with my grandchild—your child—and, of course, your father. *You did that: you killed them.* You made a terrible decision at Kavanagh's barn because of a need to be loved by your dad. And, of course, because you were drunk. Didn't you hear what Breege said yesterday? Didn't you hear how much she has suffered because of what you did? And you, through me, need to atone for that.'

'What are you saying? You're my vessel?'

'If you want to call me that, fine, but please know that I am happy to be that for you because even if I hadn't convinced Teddy to allow me to take the blame, I would be living this horrible, suffocating, crippling pain anyway. That's what mothers do—maybe not my mother, but the rest of us. We feel our children's pain more than we feel our own. And that's the sacrifice we make when we bring you into the world. And I know you're suffering deeply, my love. And not only for those three deaths but for allowing me to go to prison. Every time we've spoken since that night, I hear it in your voice—you're a changed man. But that's why I must do this penance, as my mother might call it. For us. *For them.*'

'It won't bring any of them back, Mam.'

'You're right, but there's no rule about how best to handle a tragedy like this. Living in some mansion overlooking golden beaches in the Algarve and sipping on

Dom Pérignon isn't the way to ask forgiveness for what happened. The wonderful life of Connie Maguire! No. That beautiful fiancée of yours, who lost her life because she refused to leave your side, deserves more. Much more.'

'When do you think you'll allow yourself to finish this "penance" on my behalf?'

'I don't know,' she replies softly, walking down the steps and entering the chilly waters. 'Not today.'

'Mam, what are you doing?' Liam asks, alarmed.

Connie lies on her back, her arms and legs outstretched on either side like a star. As the water washes over her face and the blood seeps through the bandages, Connie opens her right hand. The pills and tablets float on the surface and float in the direction of the rising sun. One day, Connie knows the burden she shares with her son will also fade in the direction of the rising sun. One day, she will cry. And one day, she will be ready to rejoin the world, rejoin her son. One day, she will re-learn to live again without Jess in her life.

Just not today.

ACKNOWLEDGEMENTS

THIS BOOK IS dedicated to my parents, who made every sacrifice imaginable to ensure my siblings and I received every opportunity. They also instilled a love of storytelling in us, whether it was my mother bringing us to the library every week or my father recalling a hum-drum event with the drama of a three-act opera.

Family is central to *The ~~Wonderful~~ Life of Connie Maguire*. During the writing process, many members of my family sadly died, including my aunt, Gina Trench, my godfather, Joe Smith, and my sister, Deirdre. Your passing will shape our lives forever.

I am so thrilled to collaborate with Mercier Press once again. At thirteen, I performed in a production of John B. Keane's *Sive* with my speech and drama class, directed by Patricia Molloy. I vividly remember looking at the cover of the play and seeing Mercier's logo. Little did I think that, years later, I would be a part of the Mercier family. Thank you to the many wonderful people involved in the book's production: Dee Collins, Mary Feehan, Carina McNally, Fiachra McCarthy and Katie Meegan (Cuala Creative). A special word to all the independent bookstores, the lifeblood of our communities.

An elephantine thank you to all the friends and colleagues who read drafts of this manuscript: Mary Bradford, Alexander Fitzgerald, Vanessa Keogh, Richard Murray, Déaglán Ó Donnchú and Stephen Wall. Your kindness, honesty, and insights inspired me to push myself further. In particular, I must acknowledge the incredible support of my dear friend and agent, Lorraine Brennan, who read five drafts of this manuscript and, in her unique way, convinced me I could do better. I hope I have.

A word of gratitude to my many editors in media, who have afforded me incredible opportunities to improve my craft over the years: Áine Toner, Norah and Carissa Casey, Alexander Fitzgerald, Aisling O'Toole, Esther McCarthy, Jennifer Stevens and Róisín Healy.

Thank you to all my friends and colleagues, old and new, who have supported me as an author since making my debut with *Sister Agatha: The World's Oldest Serial Killer* in 2016: Marie Bheag Breathnach, the late Eileen Canavan, John Donohoe, Christina Edge, Louise Ferriter, Emily Hourican, Wendy Logue, Gillian McCarthy, Ruth McGill, Eimear McKeever, Gary Murphy, Bairbre Ní Chaoimh, Máire Ní Mhaille, Anthony Morris, Gayle Norman, Eamonn Norris, Thea O'Brien, Darragh O'Donoghue, Patrick O'Donoghue, Sinéad O'Donnell, Noel O'Regan, Sharon Pickrel, Chrissie Poulter, Deirdre

Roberts, my former *Ros na Rún* family, the late Karl Shiels, Kemberlee and Peter Shortland, Standún (Spiddal), Angela Steen, Don Jimmy Tormey and Jennifer Zamparelli. And especially my best friend, Ruth Keane, and partner, Gabriele Bianchi. And, of course, my cats, Agatha, Poirot and the late Prince: thank you for the company and the many distractions.

Finally, I want to express my sincere gratitude to the courageous people who shared their professional and personal insights about addiction and mental health wellbeing with me. I hope this book can, in some small way, help remove the stigma.